Memoirs of a Sidekick

To Ben – a true lover of the arts

Kids Can Press acknowledges the financial support of the Government of Ontario, through the Ontario Media Development Corporation's Ontario Book Initiative; the Ontario Arts Council; the Canada Council for the Arts; and the Government of Canada, through the CBF, for our publishing activity.

Published in Canada by
Kids Can Press Ltd.
25 Dockside Drive
Toronto, ON M5A 0B5

Published in the U.S. by
Kids Can Press Ltd.
2250 Military Road
Tonawanda, NY 14150

www.kidscanpress.com

Edited by Shana Hayes
Designed by Marie Bartholomew
Cover illustration by Josh Holinaty

This book is smyth sewn casebound.
Manufactured in Shenzhen, China, in 3/2016 by C & C Offset

CM 16 0 9 8 7 6 5 4 3 2 1

Library and Archives Canada Cataloguing in Publication

Skuy, David, 1963–, author
    Memoirs of a sidekick / David Skuy.

ISBN 978-1-77138-568-8 (hardback)

        I. Title.

PS8637.K72M46 2016   jC813'.6   C2015-907091-0

Kids Can Press is a *forus*™ Entertainment company

Memoirs of a Sidekick

OF A

David Skuy

 KCP FICTION

PART I

Operation S.O.S.
versus
Rule the School

CHAPTER ONE

Boris is in a difficult situation, which means I am, too, but that's what happens when you're Boris Snodbuckle's best friend and number-one sidekick. Like two weeks ago when we snuck onto the roof of the school during a rainstorm to recreate Benjamin Franklin's lightning experiment. It got awkward when the police showed up, and … well … you get the idea.

Our current difficulties started when I suggested to Boris that we get a sip of water. Mr. Grisham, our gym teacher, had just announced a dodgeball game. Dodgeball is not kind to me. It tends to show off my lack of coordination and dread of getting smacked by a rubber ball. I hoped a bit of water would settle my nerves.

"I'm parched," I said to Boris.

We'd spent most of the class hanging out in the gym waiting for Mr. Grisham to get off his phone. He then sent us out to jog around the school a few times — for what Mr. Grisham said was track-and-field training. Boris and I went hard at it. Most everyone else walked. Boris is a bit of a fitness nut.

"Sure thing, Adrian. We might miss the first dodgeball game, though."

This was a risk I was willing to take.

"Mr. Grisham, can Adrian and I go get some water?" Boris asked.

"Okay, Buckle. Go for it. But hurry back. I want you boys in the first game," Mr. Grisham said. He offered us a wide grin, of the ear-to-ear variety. It made him look like an alligator — with a whistle around its neck.

He terrified me.

Boris put his hands on his hips. "Mr. Grisham, I know my name is kinda funny, but if you have to use a nickname, I go by the B-Ster."

I held my breath. As a gym teacher, Mr. Grisham has considerable influence among the athletic kids at Bendale Public School, and if he agreed to use the B-Ster, Boris's nickname prospects might improve.

A name like Snodbuckle practically begs for a nickname. Buckle is obvious. Unfortunately, Boris has been given some less flattering handles, such as Snod Bod, Buckle-Bottom, Snuckle-Buckle, Buckle Head and Belt Buckle. Snot-Buckle was popular in fifth grade, only to be replaced by the most hated name of all, Buckle Butt, which became all the rage last year.

My hopes were dashed when Mr. Grisham began laughing, hyena-like, for a very uncomfortable twenty seconds.

"That's a good one, Buckle," Mr. Grisham said, glancing at his phone. "Grab your water and get back here. We don't have a lot of time."

A lump formed in my throat — and a distressing gurgling feeling made itself felt in the bottom of my stomach. These were the first stages of dodgeball terror — but I kept it to myself. Boris had more important issues to deal with. As you can imagine, our classmates took Mr. Grisham's comments as an invitation to shower Boris with insults.

Inspiration struck Robert Pinsent at just the wrong time.

"Let's call him the Smell-Ster, or maybe the Bore-Ster," he said to great laughter.

Boris is Robert's opposite. Boris has deep, dark black hair, which he wears short and brushed to the side, and is of medium height, not short but shorter than the taller seventh graders. Most remarkable are the Snodbuckle eyes, alive, intense, wise — taking everything in. For reasons unclear to me, however, his kindness, compassion, charisma and intelligence have not made Boris a popular kid at Bendale. That honor has fallen to Robert, who sits at the top of the social pecking order. He is taller than Boris, a tremendous athlete and his long, wavy blond hair and perfect white teeth are a stark contrast to Boris's sharper features. Perhaps Robert's most irritating quality is his ability to get whatever he wants — without working for it — without knowing much about anything — and with annoying consistency.

Robert recently declared his intention to run for president of the student council next month. I don't believe Robert cares about the school or his fellow students, so the reasons for his declaration escape me. I shudder to think of eighth grade with a person like him at the helm.

"How about Lob-Ster or Loch Ness Dump-Ster?" said Michael Beverley, my personal nemesis and lifelong foe. He had been riding Robert's coattails for years. He'd recently decided to adopt the low-rider jean and baggy sweatshirt look to enhance his image as a tough kid, and as usual, he needed to add his two cents' worth.

Mr. Grisham's grin threatened to split his face in two.

"I really do need that water," I whispered to Boris.

Boris's shoulders slumped slightly. "Yeah, me too."

We left the gym to the sound of laughter ringing off the walls.

Boris held the door open for me.

"Do we have to play dodgeball every class?" he said. "Most of the games are like target practice. I think Grisham likes to see Robert and his crew stomp us."

Robert's crew also included Wong, tall, broad-chested, always wearing a backward baseball cap and the fastest kid in school; Henson, a rather large, muscular boy for his age, as in twelfth-grade large, who I suspected might already be shaving; and Daniels, the shortest of the group, with wild red hair, a face full of freckles and a venomous personality. Together they were the best athletes in seventh grade, and Mr. Grisham often grouped them into one team.

"And did you see those guys hogging the swings again at recess?" Boris continued. "The little kids couldn't get near them. They've totally taken them over — almost every day. Mr. Hurley was on yard duty and I told him, but he said he was too busy working on his musical. I tried to talk to the Principal about it three times this week. He keeps saying he'll talk to me later."

I was hardly surprised Mr. Hurley couldn't help. He was the head of the drama department, and for most of the year he'd been working on what he told us was going to be the most revolutionary, exciting, fantastic, magnificent play in the history of theater. I believe the working title is *Genghis Khan and Flipity-Dipity Rabbit — The Musical*.

The Principal's inaction was more distressing. Lately it's been very difficult to make an appointment with him to discuss serious school matters. Only last week he'd said, "Snodbuckle, seventh grade is over in three months. Then you just have to get through eighth grade and we're done. Let's say goodbye at your graduation and leave it at that."

It's impossible to know exactly when Boris and the Principal's relationship went off the rails. If pressed, I'd say it began in second grade when Boris was in his circus phase and tried to ride down the main school stairs on his unicycle. Boris never blamed him for his broken arm, but apparently the Principal got into some trouble with the school board and the insurance company, and since then he's remained convinced Boris is trying to ruin his career.

Nothing could be further from the truth. Admittedly, there have been a few incidents that have contributed to the Principal's aversion to Boris's company ... but back to the matter at hand.

Boris waved at the fountain for me to go first. "I don't wanna sound like a whiner, but things are messed up at Bendale. How many indoor recesses are we gonna have? It's almost two or three a week. We spend so much time in those classrooms, I think my head's gonna explode.

"I've been at Bendale for almost seven years," he continued, "and every year's the same. No running in the schoolyard; we can't play in the field if it rains or if there's snow, as if we'll drown or freeze to death. Other than Ms. Crimpet, who practically does everything herself — and I guess Mr. Hurley, who does the school play — the teachers don't run any extracurriculars. The teachers give us detentions all the time. Nothing gets better. I'm sick of it."

I let him have his turn at the fountain.

School is more a question of survival for me than it is for Boris. Never having achieved what you would call "popularity" — or made what you would call "friends," except for Boris — I do not usually worry about those types of issues. He was right, though — about all of it, and especially about Ms. Crimpet. She helped with the Science Club, the school play, the Science Fair, the volleyball team, the Green Goblins Environmental Club, the cross-country team, the junior choir ... and I heard she was organizing the Kids for a Better Tomorrow Society.

That was about it for activities at Bendale.

"It's always been like this, hasn't it?" I asked.

"Well, it's not the way it should be. Why can't Bendale change? We have one more year here. I don't wanna waste it — life's too short. We gotta do something," he said.

"I guess ... but what?"

It wasn't a particularly helpful question, but it was all I could offer.

Boris took a final slurp. "Don't know, Adrian. But something. Nothing we've tried has worked. Remember Operation Toy Drive or Operation Healthy Eats?"

Both were excellent examples. In sixth grade, Boris tried to organize a toy drive at Christmas to help needy families. We collected a straw, two broken coffee mugs and a soccer ball — with a hole in it. But the low point might have been when Boris and I protested against the cafeteria's selling fried food. We were pelted with french fries, hot dogs and burgers.

We made our way back to the gym. The door hadn't closed completely. "Not everything is bad," I said. "At least we won't have to push the door open."

I have a tendency to be overly serious. Boris has encouraged me to try to make the occasional humorous comment. I'm not sure I hit the mark this time. Boris raised his eyebrows and pursed his lips, but I didn't get the kind of reaction that typically follows any joke from Robert or Michael ... or anyone else.

"We have to do something," Boris muttered. "We can't leave Bendale like this."

Boris was in full deep-thinking mode, so I kept quiet and let him ponder — and for the briefest of moments let myself believe that maybe — just maybe — Boris would figure out a solution.

Because if Boris Snodbuckle can't solve a problem — that problem can't be solved.

CHAPTER TWO

Boris stopped abruptly as he reached for the door, as if frozen in place by Jack Frost himself. I bounced off his shoulder, and before I could ask, Boris put a finger to his lips.

"When you're prez, we're gonna run this school, bro," I heard Michael say.

I peered over Boris's shoulder and, through the crack in the door, saw Robert and his crew huddled against the gym wall.

"It'll be so freakin' sweet," Robert said gleefully. "We'll do whatever we want, whenever we want. Student council collects the money from the Fall Fair and the pizza lunches. It's going right into new phones and video games for us, and — we're gonna be going to a lot of football and baseball and hockey games with that cash. We'll sit wherever we want in the lunchroom, and the little brats will have to give us their desserts — 'cause of our hard work ..."

"Working hard eating their food," Michael cackled.

"And you know the room the aftercare program uses to store toys and equipment? I'll say the council needs it for meetings," Robert continued. "It'll be our private clubhouse. And say goodbye to stupid assemblies — I'll invent a reason for us not to go — and goodbye to those lame community activities the do-gooder losers try to get us to do, like when that dweeb Snod Crunkle made us sort food at that food bank or when we had to plant new trees for the school's playground. Total waste of time."

"Totally lame," Michael said.

"We should get Buckle Knuckle in trouble with the Principal. He gets suspended again and no one will listen to him or his plans. I'm sick of him getting in my way. Remember last year when we had those kids doing our homework until he found out? He was actually gonna turn us in unless we stopped!" Robert bristled.

"Still don't know what Buckle Knuckle meant about the Code and Rule Five and that he didn't want to tattle but he had to if we kept *bullying* those kids," Michael fumed.

"When I'm president, it'll be all about us," Robert declared. "I got it all figured out." He tilted his head and flashed his sparkling white teeth.

"We got it made, bro."

"We're gonna rule the school, baby! Who's the king of getting what he wants?" Robert said.

"We are!" Michael said, throwing a fist in the air.

"Well ... I am," Robert said to him.

"Yeah, I meant that ... You ... and us ... a bit," Michael said.

"Getting elected will be easy. All we gotta do is promise whatever people want," Robert said. "So ask around and figure out what I need to say. Even talk to the losers. I'll need their votes, too."

"Like even Snuckle Buckle?" Michael asked.

"I'm not that desperate," Robert said.

He and Michael high-fived, as Wong, Henson and Daniels laughed heartily.

Boris turned to meet my gaze. I was in complete shock — of the comatose variety. Boris remained silent and still, but his reaction came from steely-nerve determination.

Eyes slightly closed, but firm, sharp and alive, his jaw set and fists clenched — this was the B-Ster in full-focus mode.

He nodded to me and pushed the door open and walked into the gym. I followed.

"Hey, Buckle Brain," Robert said. "You're on the other team. You, too, Nickels. Hurry up. I need to throw a ball at your faces."

"Yeah, me too. I gotta throw a ball at your faces," Michael said.

Boris crossed his arms. "I hear you're running for student council president," he said to Robert.

Robert shrugged.

"I wanted to wish you good luck," Boris said, extending a hand.

Check what I said earlier about being in shock. This time my shock was like being hit by a bolt of lightning, turned into ashes, ground into powder, fed into a blender and then washed down the kitchen drain.

Robert seemed surprised, too. Wide-eyed, he accepted Boris's hand. Then the old Robert roared back into action. "When I'm president, you can carry my backpack between classes." He slapped his forehead. "I'm being stupid. You'll be too busy being lame and trying to help save some kitten from a tree. Do you ever get tired of being the school dweeb?" he said.

"Well … sure, it was embarrassing when I climbed that tree to save the kitten and couldn't get down and the fire trucks had to come. Anyway — let the best man win," Boris said. "Whoever wins, you or me, we should agree to work together — to make Bendale a great place to go to school."

Robert choked slightly. "What do you mean, you or me …?"

"I'm running for president, too," Boris said.

I joined in on the choking — and realized that I had again managed to be even more shocked.

Basically, I'd forgotten my name and my shoe size.

"You?" Michael spluttered. "Buckle Butt?"

They stared at Boris.

I could tell instantly they were impressed by his dedication to Bendale — and that, combined with his willingness to help his fellow students, would make them finally accept him as their leader.

Or not.

Robert began to laugh first. Michael joined in quickly, falling to the floor in hysterics. Wong, Henson and Daniels fell into one another's arms, the laughter robbing them of the power to stand up straight.

The shriek of Mr. Grisham's whistle startled me. "Buckle and Nickels, you're on the other side," he bellowed. "Winner stays on, so everyone should bring it. And remember, no head shots."

His mocking expression made me think this rule might not be enforced strictly.

I looked over at our teammates: Stevie Bishop, Jonah Ferreira and Brandon Mortimer. I'm far from gifted in sports, but compared to them I'm practically an Olympian.

The five of us against Robert and his pack of attack dogs?

It would be a slaughter.

"Hey, let's smoke the Snuckle with all three balls at once," Robert said.

"And then Nickels," Michael said. "Please? We gotta make him cry. It's a dream of mine."

I feared his dream was going to be my reality.

"Good luck in the election," Robert called out to us, as he and his friends took their positions.

"You can sit this one out," Boris said to me. "But I can't let Stevie, Jonah and Brandon go into battle alone."

I considered faking a serious injury — fainting came to mind — or maybe an outright heart attack.

Then I considered Boris's remarkable courage. Did he retreat from danger? Did he worry about his personal safety?

"I'm with you," I said, hoping my quivering voice didn't give away my terror.

I followed him to the far side of the gym, ignoring the "dweebs" and "losers" cascading from the bleachers.

Many centuries ago, Titus Livy wrote in his history of the Roman Empire that "being a general calls for different talents from being a soldier," which I take to mean that some people are born to lead and others to follow. I have always known Boris belonged in the first category. Then there's Stevie Bishop. Stevie suffers from a density of brain that prevents him from thinking above the level of a chimpanzee (no disrespect to chimpanzees intended, by the way). Little wonder that he tried to take charge.

"There are three balls," Stevie said to us. "Three of us will rush and two will play defense. That way we'll get a couple of balls to start, and also have reserves in case a ball chaser gets hit."

"That's a fantastic plan; I like it," Boris said. "It would work, except maybe not against guys like Pinsent, Beverley, Wong, Henson … and Daniels, on account of they are way faster than any of us and will get all the balls first. Our chasers will get out for sure, and then it's five against two and we'll be done for."

"You suck," Stevie replied.

Boris wisely offered up his own strategy. "We should hang back. Let them make the mistakes. They'll be all crazed and hyper, and maybe they'll make a bad throw and we can catch a couple. The key is to survive the first charge."

"Wuss strategy, Buckle Butt," Stevie said. "Everything you do is a disaster. We gotta attack."

"Yeah," Jonah chimed. "We gotta attack."

Brandon remained silent and very pale, his face so drained of blood he looked positively deathly. I knew Brandon from our days in the Green Goblins Environmental Club. He was a nice kid, clever but timid, and therefore unlikely to voice an opinion on the matter. I could also see that dodgeball terror had taken possession of his soul, which I know from personal experience makes it hard to speak.

18

"I really don't think your idea will work," Boris said. "Why don't we try —"

"I'm no wuss," Stevie said.

"I'm no wuss either," Jonah said.

Apparently, this closed the matter, and Stevie and Jonah walked away. Brandon followed in a daze. And I tried to prepare my body for pain.

A few girls sat in the bleachers, presumably having finished their gym class early. Two of them, Jessica Friedman and Cinny Birchwood, were waving at Robert.

"Hi, Robert," Jessica giggled.

"Hi, Robert," Cinny giggled.

Robert flicked his head in their direction and ran a hand through his hair.

Jessica and Cinny giggled some more.

"They won't listen," Boris said to me. "We gotta go with Stevie's strategy."

"But like you said, we can't win that way," I said.

"We can't let them sacrifice themselves on the front lines alone, can we?"

I had to agree. He held out his fist. I gave it a punch with the seriousness the occasion deserved.

"Buckle Butt and Nickels, you guys hang back," Stevie said, in a whisper loud enough to be heard a block away. He knelt in a sprinter's stance.

"We attack the right flank," Boris whispered to me.

"Go!" Mr. Grisham screamed.

"Arrrgh!" our opponents cried.

Brandon froze. Stevie, Jonah, Boris and I charged, which became a problem when Robert's team captured all the balls. Jonah fell first, with a direct hit to his knee. Unfortunately, the ball rolled back to the enemy. I skidded to a halt.

"Serpentine," Boris yelled.

"I'm on it," I replied, and immediately began to retreat in an S pattern. I got back to the wall without being hit. To my horror, I turned to see Boris and Stevie trapped close to the center line. Robert looked arrogant and disdainful, Michael looked goofy, and each held a ball high overhead.

"Time for a rubber ball sandwich," Robert said.

"Stevie, run for it," Boris said.

The moment Stevie began to flee, Robert threw his ball, and Boris flung himself between the ball and Stevie, like a soldier falling on a grenade to save his comrades. I felt the prickle of a tear in the corner of my right eye.

The ball hit Boris square in the face and bounced back to Robert.

"Head shot," Mr. Grisham declared. "Doesn't count. Keep firing."

"Get Buckle Butt! Get Buckle Butt!" Jessica and Cinny chanted.

Boris is a master of improvisation, as you may have gathered. He began a series of somersaults, which worked until he got dizzy and rolled the wrong way. Michael took careful aim and let fly.

"Another head shot," Mr. Grisham ruled.

"I give up," Brandon said. He ran off.

I couldn't blame him. Boris is made of much sterner stuff, though.

"No surrender," Boris declared in defiance of the overwhelming odds. He rose to his knees.

"Then take this," Robert answered.

Two balls rebounded off various parts of Boris's body. Hard to say if it was the hit off his chin that caused him to fall. The shot to his thigh got him out. I surveyed the scene. The good news was all three balls were now on my side. The bad news was Stevie and I were the only ones on our team still in the game — that is until Stevie grabbed a ball and threw it wildly at Daniels, who reached up and caught it.

I was alone against five dodgeball warriors.

Boris cast his steely gaze in my direction. "Loft one nice and easy," he said.

At first I didn't understand. Someone would catch it. But then I got it — as if a lightbulb had actually gone off in my head.

"I'm on it, B-Ster," I said. Three long strides and I had secured a ball, and then I promptly underhanded it to Wong.

"You are so out, doofus face," Michael said.

I agreed with the first part, and I would not lower myself to respond to the second. I joined Boris on the sidelines.

"Why didn't you guys hang back?" Stevie said to us. "You dumb or something?"

"You're hopeless, Buckle Head," Jonah said. "Can't you do anything right?"

Boris chewed his lower lip, scrunched his mouth to the right and then the left, sucked his upper and lower lips into his mouth at the same time and made a suction noise.

No one can match Boris under pressure.

"We should sit," I offered.

"Buckle, off the court," Mr. Grisham barked.

I took Boris by the arm and led him away. I noticed Frieda Bowman had taken a seat by herself in the bleachers to my left. I pulled Boris to the other side. Frieda and I have a difficult relationship. I think she's the most wonderful, beautiful, smart, perfect girl in the whole world. Some may prefer Jessica's classic good looks, with her thick, wavy auburn hair, peaches-and-cream complexion and bewilderingly endless supply of clothing, or Cinny's giggly, chatty, easygoing manner, but I find Frieda more captivating than all of that. The difficulty is that she does not have feelings for me — any feelings. I suspect she has trouble remembering my name. It's been like that since we met in first grade — but I remain hopeful.

Boris marched up to the top of the bleachers and sat next to Jessica.

"You're kidding, right?" she said to him. "Loserville is that way." She pointed to the lower bleachers.

Traditionally, the upper levels are reserved for the popular kids. "I see two spots in the second row," I whispered to Boris.

Boris didn't budge.

"Gross ... and totally gross," Cinny said to us, and she and Jessica moved.

A huge cheer sounded as Robert's team began to trash their next opponent.

I took the opportunity to reflect on Boris's decision to run for president of the student council. Elections at Bendale are held in the spring to give the new council members the chance to get to know one another before the summer break. He had time to mount a campaign, but I had some doubts — several, in fact. I picked one.

"Robert is going to be very difficult to beat," I said. "He's very popular."

A look of grim determination settled over Boris. "If it was easy, I wouldn't need your help," he said. "You with me on Operation Save Our School?" He held out a fist.

I extended a fist of my own — and readied myself for another Snodbuckle adventure.

CHAPTER THREE

We had one last class after gym — the dreaded drama period with Mr. Hurley. Boris always found this class extremely frustrating, mostly because we never did anything — other than watch Mr. Hurley perform scenes and songs from his new show. Perhaps this is me, but his singing reminds me of fingernails running down a chalkboard, with the clanging of marbles in a tin can and screeching wild cats in the background. It was Friday and everyone was anxious to get the weekend started.

Mr. Hurley held his red notebook up in the air, extreme satisfaction etched on his face.

"Have you ever created something so brilliant," he gushed, "so touching, sad, funny, romantic, exciting, festive and ... full of genius? You have to hear this. Listen up, please. This is important."

He ran his finger down the page of his red notebook.

"Imagine Genghis Khan and his rabbit butler, Flipity-Dipity, are looking down from a mountaintop onto a town nestled deep in a valley ...

"Flipity-Dipity says, 'But Genghis, oh, Genghis, must we really ransack, destroy and pillage again? We've been ransacking, destroying and pillaging all day, and my feet are killing me.'"

Mr. Hurley burst out laughing. "I mean, is that not the

funniest line?" He wiped a tear from the corner of his eye. "'My feet are killing me'? I mean ..." He giggled to himself for a moment.

Then Mr. Hurley straightened up and held his red notebook out in front of him. This posture signified a song was coming. Before he began, another equally noxious sound assaulted my ears.

It was the dear friend of all kids bored in class — the fart.

Naturally, Stevie and Jonah laughed the loudest; their brains cannot resist the humor of that noise. My fellow classmates followed with a few guffaws and chuckles — even Boris allowed himself a smile, and let's face it, the fart was timely.

I sniffed the air. No odor. Clearly, it was a fake. To my right, Michael, Wong, Henson and Daniels had their heads down — trying very hard not to laugh. Robert looked extremely pleased with himself. I had no doubt Robert was the guilty party.

This was hardly the first time he'd unleashed his fake fart, and even I have to admit he's good at it.

Then things took a disturbing turn.

"Good one, Snodbuckle," Robert said. He held up his hand for a high-five.

Mr. Hurley's nose crinkled tightly, and his eyebrows angled sharply upward. "I should have known you'd be the culprit, Snodbuckle. To interrupt my song with a ... a ..."

Stevie and Jonah lost it — again.

Mr. Hurley gave them a dirty look. "You have an opportunity of a lifetime — to be taught the art of drama by a professional actor, writer, director, choreographer, musician, producer and dancer," Mr. Hurley hissed, "and you want to throw it all away!"

"I didn't —"

"Silence," Mr. Hurley thundered.

I could barely breathe. This was a disaster.

"I was sitting next to Boris," I said, "and I can assure you that he did not make any ... sounds."

"Are you calling me a liar?" Mr. Hurley said, peering down at me from over his nose.

"No, only that ... you're wrong about —"

He didn't let me finish.

"Nickels, Snodbuckle, go to the office *now*, as in immediately, and tell the Principal I expect a suspension — a long one." He slapped his thigh with his red notebook. "Such a comical, touching, tragic, sweet song — ruined. It's ... unthinkable." He held the back of his hand to his forehead.

Stevie and Jonah laughed again.

"Begone with you both — straight to the Principal's office," Mr. Hurley said to us.

I was about to protest when Boris shook his head at me and rose to his feet. "No point," he said. "Come on."

Enraged by the injustice, I got up.

Mr. Hurley began to sing.

In a little town called Gilgabish,
Where the people like to eat big fried fish ...

I fairly ran out of the room.

My parents would not be happy about a suspension. Another one. Another one this month. The first came after Boris decided to test the fire hoses as a safety measure. He considered it our duty to figure out how far the water sprayed in case we had to fight a real fire. That made sense to me but not to the Principal, and he suggested a day of reflection at home. Our second suspension followed Boris's decision to repaint the library mint green, which he thinks encourages reading. Boris believes students today don't read enough. Again, the Principal strongly disagreed, and he warned us that our next suspension would be more serious.

"I'm sorry you got wrapped up in this," Boris said.

"I couldn't just sit there," I fumed. "Do you really think we'll be suspended?" I said. I decided to leave out the "again."

He held out a fist, and I promptly responded with mine.

"Probably, but I don't think it'll be more than a day," he said. Nothing gets Boris down for long. "Let's go get suspended, and then we can get to work on Operation S.O.S."

CHAPTER FOUR

We passed under the big maple tree and made our way across the parking lot to the bike racks. The meeting with the Principal had gone as Boris predicted. We'd had to wait around in the Principal's office until drama class ended for Mr. Hurley to join us, and he told the Principal what he thought we'd done. The Principal ignored our pleas of innocence and invited us to stay home on Monday to consider the pain Mr. Hurley had suffered from such an insensitive act.

I found it one of the more pleasant suspension meetings to date. We were getting good at them, I supposed.

"At least school's over," Boris said. "And we have a three-day weekend to start organizing the operation."

I looked for Boris's bike since his is easier to pick out than mine and we always park next to each other. The bright red banana seat alone made Boris's bike unique, not to mention the crimson and gold frame, the orange handlebars and the extra-large front wheel. Mine paled in comparison. It had the terrible disadvantage of being brand-new and having twelve gears, so I constantly had to hit the brakes or I would speed way ahead.

"Check that Gordie is secure?" he requested.

I checked the rope. Gordie is Boris's wagon, a gift from his parents on his fifth birthday. He rarely went anywhere without him. While Gordie might have been in need of a paint job, and one corner was bent badly and the two back wheels wobbled, he had proven his worth countless times, and we considered him a noble creature.

"What's the plan, B-Ster?"

He squeezed the fox-head horn on his handlebars. "To the War Room!" he declared.

In my enthusiasm I pedaled too hard and was soon ninety feet in front. A little pressure to the hand brake corrected the situation, and we arrived together at Boris's house.

"My folks aren't here," he said, "but we should use the window anyway — for the practice."

There have been times in the past when stealth was required, and we used the elm tree outside the window of Boris's bedroom, a.k.a. the War Room, to enter and exit. We walked our bikes to the back of the house and began to climb. I am no fan of heights, and the climb always unnerves me, so I was greatly relieved when I felt the War Room's carpet under my feet.

Boris grabbed a black marker from his desk and took a deep sniff. "The smell's almost gone, but it's all we've got." He handed me the marker and pointed to the wall. "Write down Operation S.O.S."

The best that can be said of Boris's penmanship is that it's impossible to read. He writes too fast. Boris says his thoughts tumble out too quickly and he can't help it. I wrote the heading, as instructed.

"Whoever gets the most votes is student council president, right?" Boris said.

I agreed.

Boris bowed his head solemnly. "Adrian, I don't really understand why, but ..." He leaned closer. "I sometimes get the feeling most people don't like me at school," he said, almost in a whisper. "We need to figure out how I'm going to win the election. Robert Pinsent practically runs the school. Who will vote for me?"

"Lots of kids don't really know you," I said. "Robert will probably get a lot of votes from the seventh graders and all the athletes, but to be president you have to get votes from every grade. I bet a lot of kids won't vote just based on popularity. You prove to those kids that you're going to make things better at Bendale, and I'm sure they'll cast a vote for Boris Snodbuckle — or at least maybe they will."

Boris looked at the wall momentarily. "Can you write this out underneath the heading?"

He rattled off five groups of kids at Bendale:

1. Little kids
2. Nature lover kids (Green Goblins)
3. Artsy kids
4. Brainiac kids
5. Popular kids

"There are eight grades at Bendale," Boris said. "Too many for me to get involved with individually, and kids don't hang out with only their own grades. What if we divided the kids into these five groups, and I joined their clubs or did activities with them after school? Did things to show I really want to help?"

"Sounds like a plan."

"We'll go after each group, one at a time. The last one will be the hardest because popular kids don't listen too well. I figure we'll start with the little kids 'cause I have a great idea already," he said. "We've gotta win the swings back for them. It's totally not fair. We'll need Gordie, of course."

No surprise there.

"Here's what we gotta buy — or borrow," Boris said. He dictated another list to me.

- Duct tape (2 rolls)
- Balloons (3 packs)
- Stretchy bands (x 6)
- Gum (2 packs)
- Cheesies (2 bags)
- Large bag of chips and drinks
- Candy necklaces (x 2)
- Hamburger, fries and milkshake
  from the Burger Pit (x 2)

Some of these items made sense; others were a mystery. But I had no objection to cheesies, candy necklaces, gum or chips, and I was always up for grub at the Burger Pit.

A voice from downstairs interrupted us.

"Boris!"

The distinct sound of stomping feet on stairs followed. Boris took the marker from me, wrote a dollar sign on the wall and flicked his eyebrows toward the door.

The door opened.

"There's writing on the wall," Boris's dad said.

We agreed.

"How did Adrian get in here?" he asked.

"Not sure what you mean, Dad? How do you think?" Boris said.

He stared at us.

We stared back.

"I got a call from your good friend the Principal. What's this about you disrupting class?"

Boris explained the incident with Mr. Hurley. Then he told his dad he'd decided to run for student council president.

"Well, I'm happy that you're running. That's great, but …"

The word hung in the air for some time.

"Your mom is at a meeting," his dad finally said. "No more writing on the walls, no leaving the house and no using power tools."

"Understood," Boris said.

"Absolutely, sir," I said.

I saw no reason why we couldn't follow these rules. We'd been living with the power tool ban since last summer when Boris sawed the kitchen table in half to test his theory that you could stack furniture to make your house feel bigger.

His dad eyed Boris carefully — for a long time.

"Maybe you could try not getting suspended … again … this month?" he said, in a hushed tone.

"I'll try, Dad," Boris said. "Running for president might help with that. Can you lend me some money for my election campaign? I can pay you back from my allowance."

"How much?" his dad asked.

Boris glanced quickly at the wall. "Forty-seven dollars should do it."

I had no idea politics was so expensive.

His dad took out his wallet and gave Boris fifty dollars. There was a final long look, and then he left. Shortly after that, I climbed down the tree and returned home for dinner.

PART II

Operation Swing Back

CHAPTER FIVE

I arrived at Boris's house promptly at six thirty in the morning, as agreed, just in time to see him climbing down from the War Room. He wanted an early start to set up for Operation Swing Back. He pointed at his next-door neighbor's backyard.

"I stashed my bike and Gordie in his storage shed so we could get away without waking my parents. Be careful with Chaz, though."

Chaz was the neighbor's dog, and he'd taken the oddest dislike to Boris. Granted, there was Operation Catapult to consider. While testing the catapult, we had misjudged the distance of a few water balloons and frightened poor Chaz. We felt terrible about it, but Chaz remains stubbornly convinced that Boris did it on purpose and barks ferociously at the sight of him. Boris's good nature and kindness will win Chaz over in the long term.

Chaz let out a quiet bark when he saw me but did nothing to suggest violent intent. I relaxed and pulled Boris's bike and Gordie from the shed and walked them to the street.

"Sorry for not coming over this weekend," I said. "My parents were unhappy about the suspension — and the Principal called."

The silver lining to my weekend at home was I had

time to get started on my herb garden and do more work on my Science Fair exhibit.

"My mom said there have been a lot of calls …"

Boris nodded slowly. "I get ya."

"My parents spent the weekend telling me I had to listen to teachers, show respect and not cause trouble," I said. "I tried to explain that I don't ever want to cause trouble — and that you didn't fart — that it was Robert. They kept telling me that if it was Robert, I should've told Mr. Hurley or the Principal."

"Didn't you tell them about the Code? It was a classic Rule Five. We couldn't."

"Tried to. They weren't really in a listening mood."

Boris put his hand to his heart. With his impeccable sense of timing, he knew it was the perfect moment to recite the Code. We began in unison:

1. Don't break school rules, unless there's a really good reason.
2. Never miss the opening night of an awesome action movie.
3. Eat vegetables — but you don't have to like them.
4. Try your absolute best not to lie.
5. Don't tell on kids — ever — unless you're getting them out of trouble.

The Code — the guiding principle of our lives. We'd written it in fourth grade. Contravening the Code was unthinkable.

Boris gave his fox-head horn a squeeze. "Robert keeps getting away with stuff, and I really wanted to tell Mr. Hurley the truth — I almost did when the Principal said I was the most difficult student in the history of mankind — but the Code's bigger than me getting yelled at by the Principal."

"We didn't break the Code," I said. "That's the important thing. And you know what, I think you can win the student council election — you have one vote for sure!"

Boris smiled gratefully. "Thanks. One vote's better than none." He got on his bike. "I was thinking of going with the name Big Daddy for Operation Swing Back," Boris said.

"Sounds … interesting," I said. "I'll be Firefly."

A fist bump confirmed our code names.

It would be up to Big Daddy and Firefly to free the swings for the little kids.

I hopped on my bike, and we started off down the street, Gordie squeaking and bouncing behind.

"You really gotta get that bike tuned up. It's totally out of control," Boris called out from behind me.

I applied pressure to my hand brakes.

CHAPTER SIX

I've always been the nervous type.

I remember crying in terror when my mom put me on a merry-go-round for the first time when I was three — and possibly again when I was eight. So it was no surprise to me that my chest was pounding through my rib cage as we waited to begin Operation Swing Back. Everything was ready, and the seventh graders were hogging the swings at recess, as expected.

Boris showed no signs of worry, and I tried to imitate his carefree air.

"This is it, Firefly — showtime," Boris said. "Remember — the little guys are depending on us."

"I don't think they know what we're doing, so how can they be depending on us, Big Daddy?" I said, in a last, somewhat desperate attempt to postpone the operation.

"Is anyone else doing anything?" Boris said.

He was right, of course.

Boris's smile was hopeful. "I can do this by myself," he said. "No point in both of us —"

With a firm grip on Gordie's handle, I interrupted with as much boldness as I could muster. "The school needs Boris Snodbuckle as president — and so do I. I'm ready."

We shook hands solemnly. Boris snuck out from under the slide and went over to the teeter-totter. He stuck his finger in his ear — the signal! I pulled Gordie over. Boris untied the garbage bag Gordie was carrying and looked in.

"How many water balloons do we have?" he said.

"Fifteen, Big Daddy. I added five more, just to be safe," I said.

He considered this new development. "I'll be lucky to get off that many, but a few extra can't hurt. Good work, Firefly. You organize the first, second and third graders and take your position. The start signal is a fist raised over your head."

"Good luck, Big Daddy," I said.

"We make our own luck," Boris declared.

I had to shake hands again, inspired as I was by his words. Boris must have sensed this, for he offered his hand readily. I then hustled over to the slide. Last night I had to hack into the school's computer system to find the kid with the most detentions and late slips in the primary grades. We knew that broke the rules, and we felt bad. Boris and I discussed it at length. Ultimately, we determined that Rule One permitted me to do it — this one time — and I made sure to limit my search very narrowly ... just detentions and late slips. The success of Operation Swing Back rested on our finding a primary boy or girl with real spirit and great leadership skills.

One candidate had jumped out at me — by a very wide margin — a certain Lynda Skittle, in third grade.

"Excuse me," I asked a passerby who appeared to belong to the primary grades. "Do you happen to know a student named Lynda Skittle?"

The boy snorted at the question. "Of course I do." He began to run off.

"Could you possibly point her out? I need to speak to her," I said.

"What? Are you new? She's right there," the boy said. He pointed at a girl standing on top of the slide. She was a tiny waif of a thing, with thick, curvy black hair that fell to below her shoulders. She wore a blue one-piece corduroy jumper, a hot-pink turtleneck, a pink jean jacket, striped leggings and running shoes.

"This is Skittle World," she cried with her arms raised in the air. "No one's allowed to slide without the secret password." She glowered at the crowd of kids looking up at her.

"Eat worms — get germs," a young girl whispered.

"Come up, Maggie," Lynda said.

Maggie let out a squeal of delight.

"Lynda, I need a word with you, please," I said, with the utmost politeness. I began to climb the ladder.

"First, second and third graders get the small play structure on Mondays, bub," Lynda shouted down at me. "Get off."

I paused at the top rung. I admired her feistiness but worried she might not be open to conversation.

"I realize that," I said, "but I need to speak to you about something important — something to help you and all the primary grades."

"What about?"

"I would like to discuss it in private. I'd like to come up, if I could."

"What's the password?" she demanded.

"Something about worms?" I offered. I silently cursed myself for not paying more attention.

I felt a hand tug on my pant leg.

"Eat worms — get germs," Maggie quietly said to me.

"Thanks," I told her and repeated the phrase.

"Hurry up," Lynda said. "You're wasting sliding time."

I climbed quickly. I, too, was in some haste. Recess would be over soon. I decided against small talk and got right to the point.

"Do you want to play on the swings?" I said to her.

She poked me with her finger. "Are you confused? The seventh graders use the swings now."

"What if Boris Snodbuckle got the seventh graders to leave — so you could use them, like maybe in the next couple of minutes? Could you convince some of your friends to run over and swing?"

She eyed me carefully. "Is Snodbuckle that dweeb they call Buckle Butt?"

I assured her she was terribly mistaken about the dweeb part. "Boris Snodbuckle is running for student council president, and he wants the younger grades to vote for him. He's going to get the older kids off the swings to show how much he cares about Bendale's little kids."

"I'm not a little kid! And Robert Pinsent's gonna be president. He's got the best hair in school, and Boris has a funny name," Lynda said.

I glanced nervously at my watch. Boris would be

disappointed if we had to postpone. "So tell me, can Boris count on you to rush the swings when the big kids leave?"

She shrugged. "They won't leave. But if this ... Snod Thingy can do it, like if he's got special powers or something, then okay. I'm tired of being the Slide Queen."

I was glad to hear it.

"And in the election for student council president, can we count on you and your friends to consider voting for Boris Snodbuckle?" I said.

Suddenly Lynda jumped to the side to stop an incursion coming up the slide. A single look from Lynda made the boy lose his grip and slide back to the ground.

"Wait! I'm talking," she shrieked. "And you didn't say the password."

"Lynda? Do we have an agreement?" I asked.

She scrunched her mouth to the side. "I sorta already promised Robert to get the third-grade vote for him. Robert told me he would end the Wedgie War. Michelle and Benji got pulled today."

The word *pulled* had taken on a sinister meaning recently. Two months ago, a third-grade student stomped on the toes of Sherman Thomas Sidelman, a fairly large and vindictive eighth grader. There is some question whether the foot stomping was intentional. Sidelman thought so and promptly effected a wedgie; that is, he *pulled* the poor kid's underwear from the back as high as it could go. That led to several more victims, as Sidelman went on a wedgie rampage, and despite a few stern warnings from the Principal, students were getting pulled on a regular basis.

I am somewhat ashamed to admit that I have been a wedgie victim.

Did Robert have the power to arrange a wedgie truce? He might — largely because he and his crew did a lot of the pulling.

"But the swings? Wouldn't the primaries enjoy a chance to play on them — again?"

Lynda reflected. "If that Buckle kid clears those goofs off, we'll swarm."

I had a final question. "How can I be sure the first, second and third graders will swarm?"

"You kidding? I'm the Skittle," she said.

I was impressed by her confidence.

She reminded me of a younger, and somewhat more aggressive, Boris Snodbuckle.

I extended my hand to shake on it. She stomped on my foot. I assumed that meant we had a deal.

I raised my fist.

CHAPTER SEVEN

Boris put the first water balloon into a slingshot fashioned out of stretchy bands, the kind people use for yoga. The bands had cost Boris dearly — $12.25 to be precise. The cost was totally justified when the balloon flew through the air and hit Robert squarely on the head. Boris inserted another balloon and let it fly.

"The swings should be for everyone, not just seventh graders," he shouted. Michael joined Robert in wetness. I enjoyed that.

"The swings belong to everyone!" Boris shrieked, as he let forth another volley. Two more balloons found targets. Cinny Birchwood began to cry. Jessica Friedman hopped off a swing.

"Get him," Jessica screeched.

"Get him!" Robert bellowed.

"Get him!" Michael sounded.

My chest began to pound again.

Boris, ever cool in the face of danger, fired another.

En masse they charged, at least twenty kids. I saw Boris consider a final balloon, before he wisely jumped on my bike and raced off. Once he and the raging mob turned the corner of the school, I jumped into action.

"Go for it," I yelled to Lynda.

I needn't have bothered. Practically every kid under four feet joined the promised swarm. They covered every inch of the swings, cheering and yelling lustily. My heart swelled to hear their high-pitched shrieks of joy. I would have loved to watch them frolic, but I had work to do.

I dragged a garbage can to a high fence about sixty feet due north of the swings. I then reached into the thick bush that covered the fence, pulled out a rope ladder and tested the safety rope. Boris had constructed the ladder out of materials in his father's workroom. That workroom has been a virtual treasure chest for us over the years.

The plan was simple enough. Boris was going to ride around the school to give the little kids time to swarm the swings, and then he'd climb the fence to safety. I ran back and rolled Gordie behind the large maple tree next to the parking lot. I checked my watch. In approximately twenty more seconds, Boris was scheduled to appear.

Five, four, three, two, one … Nothing.

I counted down from fifteen. Nothing. Had they caught him? That would be awful. They'd tear him apart.

At that moment, Boris appeared, on foot, from around the corner of the school. Wong, Henson and Daniels were about forty-five feet behind and Robert and Michael not far behind them, with the rest of the kids pulling up the rear.

I clutched my hair. He had to get to the fence and climb the rope ladder before they caught him. If speed were based on determination, no one would have come close. But Boris simply did not enjoy the advantage of foot speed, especially compared to Wong, a cheetah in human form.

I could barely look. He wasn't going to make it.

A flash of red streaked by. Wong slowed. Then a flash of blue crossed my line of vision, and Henson and Daniels slowed, too. I heard Lynda let out a war cry and turned to see that little cyclone manning the slingshot, assisted by her sidekick, Maggie, firing water balloons with ferocity — and remarkable accuracy. Several people took direct hits. Their bravery allowed Boris to reach the fence unhindered. He hopped onto the garbage can and climbed the rope ladder to the top of the fence. He then pulled up the ladder. I was pleased to see him tie the safety rope around his waist. He was a good fifteen feet up.

"Freedom to swing," Boris yelled, and the little kids cheered. "First, second and third graders have the right to swing," he continued, and the cheers got louder.

"We're gonna get you for this," Robert interrupted. His mob joined him in glaring menacingly.

"So climb up and get me," Boris said.

Without the rope ladder, we knew they could not. Branches from the hedge poked through the fence and created an impossible barrier.

It was a magical moment. He'd done it. The little kids had the swings. So what if things returned to normal tomorrow? The first, second and third graders would never forget this day — and neither would I.

Boris began the speech we'd prepared.

"If I'm honored by your votes and become student council president, the first, second and third grades will get the swings on Mondays and Wednesdays — at both recesses. What do you say to that?"

He thrust his fist in the air.

"Student council president?" Michael said. "You?" He turned to Robert. "I wonder if you'll get more votes than him?" he said sarcastically.

"I will if I get more than one," Robert scoffed.

As always, his insult was followed by loud laughter and a number of backslaps from his friends.

"I want to represent everyone, including the older kids," Boris said. "But you have to admit it's unfair to keep the swings from our primary friends."

I flushed with pride. I had recommended he use the term *primary friends* for dramatic effect.

"And if I'm president, Bendale will be run fairly. All kids should get a chance to play a sport — or to swing; we should have more extracurriculars; you should be able to sit anywhere you want in the lunchroom and no one should be forced to play dodgeball."

I noticed Robert eyeing the crowd carefully. He turned to face them. "This is pathetic," he said. "Buckle Beak heard me telling Michael that, as president, I would make sure younger students got their turn on the swings, and he's copying me."

"Yeah. It's pathetic," Michael parroted. "I was there. I totally remember."

Boris cannot stand liars. They offend his very soul. And it hurt him to hear some of the little kids begin to chant Robert's name. Boris shuffled along the fence to get to a better spot to continue his campaign speech. He hesitated and then took one more step to his right.

That proved to be a bad decision.

Boris fell.

Later he told me the sun was in his eyes, and I understand how distracting that can be. He said his right shoelace got tangled in the fence, which caused him to stumble, and then the safety rope got wrapped around his left foot, which didn't help with his balance.

It doesn't matter how he ended up hanging upside down. What matters is that he continued his speech. "Together we can change things for the better, like being fair about using the equipment and the field," he said.

"You're such a loser, Buck Teeth," Michael roared.

He was laughing too hard to say more. In fact, all the kids began to laugh. Even I had to admit there was a sliver of comedy.

"Have a snack," Robert said.

A pinecone set sail and caught Boris in the chest. I cursed Robert's tremendously powerful and accurate throwing arm. That was followed by a slight lull, and the laughter died away. It was immediately replaced by the bloodcurdling screams of dozens of kids throwing pinecones at Boris. Boris ducked and twisted as best he could, but despite his acrobatic attempts to escape, he suffered several direct hits. He didn't let that interrupt his speech, however.

"We will work together, ouch ... to decide the best way, oww ... working with teachers and students, oof ..."

I left my hiding spot to find help and had barely taken ten steps when the Principal came barreling toward Boris, followed by a few other teachers, including Mr. Grisham, who was talking on his phone. The attacks on Boris stopped. While we had discussed what I should do in case Boris was apprehended by the Principal or another teacher, we hadn't discussed the possibility of Boris dangling upside down from the top of the fence. I decided the two situations were similar enough, which meant my primary duty was to get Gordie to safety. As I began to pull him to the parking lot, I noticed Lynda and Maggie had left the scene and were sitting on the swings. Lynda looked rather perturbed. Maggie pointed a few times at Boris, nodding her head all the while.

I tied Gordie up and doubled back to retrieve my bike. I passed Frieda sitting by herself on a bench, but she was too immersed in her book to notice me. In the field, two kids were standing together. I ventured over.

"That's my bicycle," I said. My bike lay on the ground in front of Stevie and Jonah.

"Why did Buckle Head fall off your bike?" Jonah said.

"And why was everyone chasing him?" Stevie said. "Did he say something stupid again?"

"Hardly," I said. "He freed the swings for the primary grades and announced that he will run for student council president."

"Yeah, right — as if," Jonah said.

"He must have said something totally stupid to get everyone that mad," Stevie said. "Can't believe we missed it."

I heard the blaring siren of a fire truck as it pulled up in front of the school.

PART III

Operation Rally
in the Valley

CHAPTER EIGHT

"I'm turning myself in," I said. "This isn't fair. I was part of it, too."

Boris had been suspended after being pulled down from the fence by the firefighters. I couldn't let him take the fall for Operation Swing Back — no pun intended.

"What would that prove?" he said to me. "It was only a one-dayer, and my parents are more used to suspensions than yours. And Operation Swing Back was a success."

"It was a success for the little kids," I said. "What about for the election campaign? I can't believe Robert got away with lying. How could the Principal be so gullible as to believe Robert wanted the primary grades to have the swings Mondays and Wednesdays? It's beyond frustrating. It pains me to admit it, but he outsmarted us. I've even heard Robert's name being chanted around the schoolyard by a bunch of first graders."

I was finding Rule Five of the Code very difficult at the moment. Robert's trickery went unnoticed, and we couldn't say anything. Now Boris's hopes for election rested with the remaining four groups.

"No point getting down about it," Boris said. "The important thing is the primaries get to swing. We've still got lots of time for votes."

"Did you have a chance to think about the nature lover kids during the suspension?" I asked.

"I didn't do much else," Boris said. "The problem is most of those kids belong to the Green Goblins, and I don't think they like me too much."

"It was over a year ago that we got kicked out," I said. "Maybe they've forgotten."

"I almost got them all detentions for a week, and their field trip to Bug World was canceled," he said. "I kinda doubt it."

"You're probably right," I concurred sadly.

The six weeks we'd been members of the Bendale Green Goblins Environmental Club, run by the tireless Ms. Crimpet, had been happy days for Boris and me. The study of the impact of global warming followed by the potential imminent extinction of the hawksbill turtle inspired Boris's first environmental mission, Operation Feel the Wheel. The idea was simple enough. Boris found out that the teachers used Styrofoam cups in their lounge for coffee. Styrofoam releases harmful gases into the air and remains undecomposed in landfill sites for centuries. Drastic and immediate action was needed. Boris worked out a plan to replace the Syrofoam cups with reusable mugs. Boris and I even registered for an intensive pottery course at the community center to learn how to "throw the clay," which is fancy talk for using a potter's wheel. We finished the two-day course with three dozen oven-fired mugs for the teachers — and some new friends at the Bendale Retirement Home.

Boris invited our fellow Green Goblins to join us

on the operation, which required us to remove the Styrofoam cups, cut them into pieces and then put those pieces in the bottom of the indoor planters situated about the school. Styrofoam's indestructibility and imperviousness to water make it an excellent drainage material.

Boris and I wrestled with the question of whether we were justified in entering the Teachers' Lounge. Rule One of the Code mandated that we could not *break school rules, unless there's a really good reason.* In the end, we decided we had no choice. The environment needed us.

Unfortunately, the Principal chose to ignore that we reduced the need for more Styrofoam cups, recycled the cups we removed and left behind our ceramic mugs, including a few incorporating the Japanese kaki-yu glazing technique. Instead, he chose to focus on the fact that we had entered the Teachers' Lounge without permission. He threatened all the Green Goblins with a week-long detention. Fearless in the face of environmental challenges, the members of the club proved less courageous when it came to getting into that kind of trouble. The Principal offered them a choice — everyone got the detention, or Boris and I had to go. He also canceled Bug World.

The vote was unanimous. We were out.

Despite being kicked out, Boris begged the Principal to let the Green Goblins go to Bug World, always the highlight of the year for the club. He refused. We had obviously underestimated the teachers' attachment to Styrofoam.

"I need to do something big, something so enormous the Green Goblins will forgive me," Boris said. "I wrote out so many ideas I had to start writing on the War Room's ceiling, but then, when I was about to give up, I got a great idea while I was at the Burger Pit."

"I'm a little surprised your dad let you go to the Burger Pit when you were suspended," I said.

"He didn't exactly, but I felt bad about getting another suspension, so I bought him a Monster Manhattan Burger, fries and a strawberry shake."

I wiped away the drool from the corner of my mouth. "Where'd you get the money?"

"I did some yard work for my neighbor when Chaz was at the vet. I left a bone for him to chew on. I hope he can smell that it was from me. Anyway, I went by the Valley on the way home. Guess what I saw?" Boris said.

The Valley — a magical place with so many wonderful memories. And yet, I could barely stand to hear Boris mention it. Only last summer we'd built a tree fort there; this winter we'd cleared a bush on the east side to create a brand-new toboggan path — *Suicide Steep*. A deep forest leading to a ravine was on the south border, higher ground to the north provided a fenced-in area for our four-legged friends, and to the west was a large patch of meadow used by kids to play Frisbee, football, soccer or tag.

For Boris and me, our love affair with the Valley had hit a roadblock about two months earlier when some parents from nearby homes banned us after we'd attempted to slide down Suicide Steep on a sofa we'd found on the sidewalk. One parent said something about "the last straw," and another said, "This will end in bloodshed if we don't act fast." Boris had argued that the sofa was only going to be thrown out, that we had found it abandoned in front of number 43 and that we would have absolutely put it back. His arguments fell on deaf ears. I had not been back to the Valley since. In light of the ban, I was surprised to hear that Boris had taken such a risk.

"I can't imagine what you saw," I said. "But by now I suppose the snow will have melted in all but the deepest reaches of the ravine. Possibly some trees are beginning to sprout their first shoots of spring-green leaves. And since it has been rather warm, I bet the meadow is dotted with sparks of color from the first of the spring flowers."

Boris cast a series of raised eyebrows in my direction. "You scare me sometimes," he said. "But no, what I saw was a bunch of diggers, piles of lumber, chopped-down trees and construction materials and ..." Boris stopped. He looked grief-stricken. "They've built a model home right in the middle of the meadow for a subdivision called Pleasant Valley Estates — right in the middle!"

Overcome, he lowered his chin to his chest.

"I don't understand," I said. "Who would do that?"

"A developer! I asked my dad when I came back from the Burger Pit, and he told me a developer had bought the land to build houses. My dad said they don't care about anything but money. In a few months, the Valley will be gone — forever. I gave him his burger and he started asking me all sorts of questions, like 'How did you get this?' and 'Didn't I tell you to stay in your room?'

You know how he gets. Then it hit me. This is how we're gonna get the Green Goblin vote. We're gonna save the Valley, you and me."

I stared, wide-eyed. "How are we going to stop the developer?"

A Cheshire-cat grin spread across Boris's face. "We're not gonna give him a choice, Adrian," he said. "After school tomorrow we start Operation Rally in the Valley. Just meet me at the Valley at five o'clock sharp."

Boris often has a few last-minute details to work out with his plans, so I didn't press him. Besides, Operation Rally in the Valley affected me personally, which meant this sidekick would most definitely report for duty.

CHAPTER NINE

The next day after school, I raced home to work on my Science Fair exhibit. I recalculated the energy outputs for the solar-powered trains, sculpted three pine trees for the miniature town and finished the wood railings for a bridge that spanned an artificial river. I had just started to test the water pump when my alarm went off, reminding me it was time to go. My mother gave me strict instructions to be back by six thirty for dinner, and knowing Boris occasionally lost track of time, I worried how we would be able to save the Valley in such a short period of time.

When I saw the destruction to my precious Valley, I almost wished I hadn't come. Construction materials dotted the once pristine fields, with several vehicles parked on the ridge across the way. I heaved a sigh, and I doubt a more heavy-hearted sigh has ever been heaved. I sat to wait for Boris.

I'd barely put bottom to earth when Boris sped past on his bike, Gordie bouncing behind. He skidded to a stop behind a mass of bushes and jumped off, lying prone on the ground. "Adrian, get down! We're on ultra-super maximum alert," he whispered.

I immediately hit the dirt, as the expression goes, and slithered over to him on my stomach.

"What are we doing?" I asked.

"Step one — observe the enemy and supply the tower," Boris said. He pulled a pair of binoculars from his backpack and surveyed the Valley. He gave them to me. "Our target is Tower One," Boris said. "We have to infiltrate enemy territory and deliver supplies to Tower One without being seen. The entire operation depends on it."

I could see one or two men milling about. Perhaps most of the workers had gone home. "Maybe it's time we discussed Operation Rally in the Valley?" I said, in a suggestive tone. "For example, what's Tower One — and what's the enemy territory — and what supplies do we need?"

"Roger that," Boris said. He pulled some face paint from his backpack and began rubbing it on his face. "Tower One is our tree fort. Enemy territory is the Valley, since the developer owns it now. The enemy agents are the construction workers. We gotta carry food and water, and a few other things, into Tower One, so that we have stuff to eat and drink when we come back."

"We're coming back to the tree fort ... I mean Tower One? Why?"

"Operation Rally in the Valley! We're going to occupy Tower One until the developer leaves. My dad set up Twitter and Instagram accounts and a Facebook page for me. I told him it was for a school project. And it sorta is. Saving the Valley is for all the kids at school —" He looked at me. "Is that a Code violation?"

"I know you feel bad about not telling your dad everything," I said. "Rule Four of the Code states you have to try your absolute best not to lie — and that's what you did. You told as much of the truth as you possibly could under the circumstances. I don't see a Code violation."

"Thanks, Adrian. I needed that. Anyway, I'll live tweet, update the Operation Rally in the Valley Facebook page and add pictures to Instagram, and all the kids at school will join us and ..." Boris rubbed his chin with his hand. "I don't like Tower One. It's boring. Can you think of a better name?"

"How about TF One?" I offered.

"Not bad," Boris said wistfully, "but I was hoping for something a bit more ... exciting."

I put the binoculars down. Boris relied on me in these situations, and I did not want to let him down. "Maybe if I knew more about the operation?"

Boris nodded. "Here's the deal. We're going to stay in the tree fort, or Tower One, or TF One ... We really need another name. Those are bogus," Boris said with disgust. "Anyway, we're going to stay there and organize a mass protest with Bendale kids until the evil developer quits ruining the Valley."

At least now I knew the plan. I didn't have time to think about it, though. Boris was unhappy about his name for our tree fort. As a bit of a history buff, I'm fascinated by the Roman Empire, particularly the emperors Augustus and Tiberius, who ruled from 27 BCE to 37 CE. I decided to lean in that direction. "There's an expression, 'All roads lead to Rome,'" I said, "which has its origin in the time of the Roman Empire some two thousand years ago. Back then it meant every road in Europe eventually connected to a road that would lead to the city of Rome. Since the tree fort is the base of the operation, and we want everyone to come here to protest the development, how about we call the tree fort *Roma*? It's Italian for Rome."

The brightness from Boris's smile could have lit Rome itself. "Perfect. Love it. Roma it is."

"I'm curious," I said. "What's the inspiration for this operation?"

"That article you gave me about the Occupy Wall Street movement when those students sat in the streets of New York City to protest the banks. Older kids will have Facebook, Twitter and Instagram, and they'll come to help. And they'll tell the younger kids. Newspapers and television stations will come, too, I know it. The evil developer can't do any evil developing with five hundred kids in the field and television cameras everywhere. The beauty of this operation is that we save the Valley, lift our ban and maybe the Green Goblins won't hate me so much. It's a win-win-win."

I grasped him by the forearm and told him to grab mine. "This is the traditional Roman handshake," I said.

Boris immediately got into the historical theme. "We should have Roman code names, too. Whaddya got?"

"How does Octavius strike you?"

"Erfect-pay," Boris said in pig Latin.

"I'll be Flavius," I said.

Boris shoved the face paint into my hand. "Lather up, Flavius, and let's get going." His face was a muddy green. I began to smear my face as well. When I was also camouflaged, Boris took hold of his backpack and began to crawl along the hill. I grabbed the remaining bag off Gordie and followed.

Boris held up a fist, the stop signal, and took out his binoculars. "There are still two enemy agents down there, about three hundred feet away," he said. "We should belly our way across the top of the hill around to the forest on the other side of Suicide Steep, and then snake down to Roma."

"Copy that," I said.

Boris and I began to crab our way along the ground, looking up occasionally for enemy agents. It was hard going. My knees and elbows were in a sorry state by the time we got to the forest. Boris snapped to his feet, held himself in a deep squat, arms parallel to the ground and bent at right angles, eyes darting every which way, until he was satisfied we were undetected. That took a good minute. Boris then headed down toward Roma, scrambling from tree to tree. I felt somewhat like a ninja and threw in a few karate chops and kicks. At one point, Boris attempted a somersault on a steep incline and landed in a bush. Fortunately, I was there to pull him out.

When we got to the bottom of the hill, I was downright winded and light-headed. Boris showed no ill effects, despite his collision with the bush. His eyes shone brightly.

"Flavius, the target," he whispered. "I'm gonna make a run for it. I'll give a signal when I'm there and you can come."

"What's the signal?"

He considered the question at length. "I'll make a

birdcall." He took me by the shoulder. "If I get caught, Flavius, you need to save Gordie and get away yourself. We can't both go down."

"I can't abandon you," I said.

"Gordie needs you," he said.

I grasped his forearm, and he did mine. The next moment, Boris jumped back into his squat, surveyed the scene a final time and then raced toward Roma. I watched with a lump in my throat. It would be a bitter pill indeed to leave Octavius to the enemy agents.

Boris scurried up to Roma and disappeared through a hole in one of the walls that served as our door. Moments later, I heard a terrible quacking, gasping sound. Was Boris hurt? Had he been captured? Had enemy agents infiltrated Roma? I began to tiptoe back up the hill. I stopped after thirty feet and listened closely for sounds of struggle. All was silent. Now I was really confused. Had they gagged Boris to prevent him from sounding a warning? I crept back to Roma.

I was facing perhaps the most difficult decision of my life. If I walked into a trap and harm came to Gordie, Boris would never forgive me. If I ran away unnecessarily, then I would jeopardize the operation before it even began.

But what had made that bizarre noise?

I crawled to the tree and pressed against the trunk. Still no sound from inside Roma other than a slight shuffling of feet. I took a deep breath to gather my courage and headed up the ladder.

"What took you so long?" Boris asked.

"I thought you might have been caught," I said,

somewhat in shock. Boris stood in the middle of Roma — very much uncaptured. "Didn't you hear that terrible noise?"

"I didn't hear anything. Just my birdcall."

I had clearly misjudged things.

"Flavius, can you take the stuff from these two backpacks and put them in those duffel bags?" Boris said. "I gotta reorganize a bit."

"I'm on it, Octavius," I said

I pulled out a pile of comic books, a blanket, a jar of Nutella, fish crackers, a pack of cards, a fake mustache, two walkie-talkies and a yo-yo. When I'd finished, Boris greeted me with a deadly serious expression on his face. "Once we hit the ground, all hell may break loose. It'll be every man for himself. No other way." He held out his arm. "A pleasure serving with you, Flavius."

I gripped his forearm firmly.

"Wait thirty seconds and then follow," he said, before slipping out the door.

I began counting. Suddenly, my heart rose in my chest, and I held my breath. Voices! Enemy agents incoming and barely ten feet away.

"I can't get to this area until Thursday," a man said in a husky voice.

"Thursday? I can't wait that long," another man said. His voice was very nasal and high-pitched. "Why are you always behind schedule? You're costing me a fortune. I needed this tree down a week ago. I'm going to have to review the contract."

"Review the contract. You'll see that we're right on schedule, even a bit ahead," Husky Voice said.

"That's what you always say," Nasal Voice said. "Anyway, get this tree down first thing in the morning. Use the bobcats and the backhoe to clear the rest of the scrub away, and start digging trenches for sewers two, three and four. Then get moving on the roads. I want concrete pouring next week."

"I don't see why we have to cut this tree down. We can work around it. And look, the kids have made a fort," Husky Voice said.

"Easy for you to say. It costs money to work around the trees. It's a lot less expensive to knock them down and plant new ones."

"But this tree must be a hundred years old," Husky Voice said.

"Maybe," Nasal Voice said. "What can I say? Budget is tight. It's got to come down first thing tomorrow morning. Understood?"

"Yes, sir," Husky Voice said.

I heard the sound of crunching sticks under their work boots, and then the voices faded away. I took a moment to gain control of my emotions. I had to tell Boris! I poked my head out the door. Satisfied that the enemy agents were gone, I raced back to the bikes as fast as I could. Boris was practicing wheelies.

"They're going to cut it down — the tree, I mean — or Roma — tomorrow," I gasped. "I heard them."

Boris looked grim. "That leaves us no choice. We'll have to begin Operation Rally in the Valley tonight." He sighed. "Another day to organize would be better, but we can't let them chop down Roma. You should have dinner at my place."

"Dinner might be a problem. My mom is expecting me at six thirty sharp." I looked at my watch. I had fifteen minutes to make it.

"Okay. Go home for dinner, but tell her you're having a sleepover so we can work on your Science Fair exhibit."

I tried to ignore the twinge of conscience. We were skirting a violation of Rule Four of the Code. Technically, we were having a sleepover, although not for that reason. It was a tough call. But Boris needed me.

And the Valley had to be saved.

"I'll see you at seven thirty, Octavius," I said and headed for home.

CHAPTER TEN

The sun had set long ago. Fortunately, the moon still cast a glow. Boris crouched behind a burly tree and peered slowly around the trunk.

"No enemy agents," he whispered. "It's clear to Roma."

Boris went first, without the somersault this time. In keeping with this more careful approach, I kept my karate chops to an absolute minimum. Once inside, Boris took a smartphone from his pocket.

"My dad let me borrow this," he said. He took a few pictures. "I'll take more when the tree cutters come and upload them to Facebook and Instagram. I've already been tweeting. I figure every twenty minutes will be good, give or take." He looked up at me. "We can save the Valley, Flavius, and maybe, just maybe, the Green Goblins might vote for me and let us back into their club." He reached into a garbage bag and pulled out two granola bars and tossed one to me.

He'd barely taken a bite when he suddenly stood up. "Did you hear that noise?"

I had. It sounded like voices. My heart began to pound. Then Boris began to grin. My heart pounded harder. His grin grew larger.

I was confused.

"Welcome to Operation Rally in the Valley," he yelled.

I was horrified. "The enemy agents will hear," I hissed.

"Enemy agents?" Boris said. "Sandy and Ernie are friends."

A young woman approached, followed by a man holding a camera. Another woman stood several feet back. She held a leash, which was attached to a small black dog with spiky fur and a pointy nose. My knowledge of dogs is fairly encyclopedic, but I didn't recognize the breed. I assumed it was a mutt — and a cute little critter at that.

"Are you the Boris who told us about some protest, a valley rally?" the young woman said.

"I'm Boris Snodbuckle. Are you Sandy?"

"Yup. I'm the local news editor for CRUSH TV," Sandy said. "Are you really going to stay in that tree fort all night?"

"We're gonna stay until this developer agrees to stop wrecking the Valley," Boris said. "This is Adrian Nickels, by the way."

I waved.

"Do you mind if Ernie shoots some video?" Sandy asked. Ernie waved and popped a Tic Tac into his mouth.

"Go for it, Ernie," Boris said. He turned to me. "Do you have the manifesto?"

I took it from my pocket. We'd taken a minute to jot down a few words, something dramatic in case someone asked for a statement.

"I would like to start by ..." Boris paused. "Is the camera rolling?" he asked.

"Give us a second," Sandy said.

Ernie popped the Tic Tacs open, took another,

pressed a few buttons on his camera and swung the camera to Sandy.

"Sandy Quithers here for CRUSH TV with a breaking story involving two brave young boys, Boris Snodbuckle and … his friend, students from Bendale Public School. It's eight o'clock at night, and these two boys are in a tree fort, which they built themselves, in a place known to locals as the Valley. That's right. Two young children are camping out in a tree fort to voice their concerns about the proposed new Pleasant Valley Estates subdevelopment. It's an amazing story of youth social activism. Can two boys actually save what is perhaps the last untouched, old-growth forest left in our city?"

Ernie panned to us. Roma was cast in light. I waved.

"Tell us, boys, why are you doing this?" Sandy said.

Boris stared down.

"This would be a good time to read the manifesto," I whispered.

Boris cleared his throat. "Greetings, Bendale. This is Boris Snodbuckle, candidate for student council president, former member of the Green Goblins Environmental Club, and one kid who's darn angry about an evil developer destroying our Valley. Of course, people need to live in houses, but do we really need houses here? Do we need to chop down the trees? This tree is over a hundred years old! And once the houses are built, we won't be able to come and play here anymore, not with fences and driveways and roads. The forest and the Valley will be gone — forever. Where will the animals who live here go? Where will the kids of Bendale play? We need you, Bendale. We need everyone to stand up to this developer and save the Valley. So come to the Valley, right now, and join our protest. Together, we're going to occupy the Valley until the evil developer leaves. Together, Operation Rally in the Valley will save this place. So, everyone, drop what you're doing and get over here. Just ask yourself: When the Valley's gone, where will you play? When the Valley's gone, what's next?"

I mouthed the words as Boris spoke.

"Well said," Sandy said. "How long are you going to stay here?"

"As long as it takes," Boris said. "We have enough supplies for weeks. We aren't going anywhere until the Valley is safe."

I assumed Boris was being dramatic. There had been no mention of spending weeks in Roma. I couldn't blame him, though. My emotions were running high as well.

"What do your parents think of all this?" Sandy asked.

"They're one hundred percent behind us," Boris said. "One hundred and fifty percent — even two hundred percent."

"Do you have anything else you'd like to say?"

"We want everyone to come to the Valley, tonight or tomorrow, especially kids from Bendale Public School. And if you elect me as your student council president, I promise to protect the environment at school, from the trees to the tiny, hardworking ants. So if you love the Valley, if you love the environment, then you gotta come and stop this. They're planning to chop this tree down tomorrow! Tomorrow! Come on, everyone, and let's Rally in the Valley."

Boris's words thundered into the dark skies. The camera moved away from us and Roma was cast in moonlight. The lady with the dog walked off.

Ernie turned the camera back to Sandy. "Two boys are calling on Bendale to join them in protest against the destruction of the Valley. It's boys against the forces of development and money. Who will win?" She paused. "This is Sandy Quithers reporting for CRUSH TV. Back to you, Sabrina." The camera light turned off. "I think that's good," Sandy said. "Thanks, Boris … and Boris's friend. We'll run this story for the ten o'clock news. Good luck."

Ernie waved his Tic Tacs at us. They left — and we were alone.

Boris puckered his lips and made several suction noises. "You want chips and onion dip?" he said.

There was only one answer to that question.

CHAPTER ELEVEN

A tremendous roaring sound woke me up. I sat up in terror thinking I was about to plunge over Niagara Falls. Fortunately, I was completely dry, which convinced me I was in no immediate danger. My relief was short-lived, however. The roaring sound was a chain saw!

I crawled over to Boris. "Octavius! Get up!" He continued sleeping. "Octavius, they're here. They have a chain saw. They're going to cut Roma down."

Boris sat up. "Huh?"

He isn't usually at his best when he first wakes up.

"Chain saws," I said. "Roma will fall."

In a flash he was up — and then fell flat on his face. "Stupid sleeping bag," he said, kicking himself free. "You can't cut this tree down — you tree cutter!" Boris yelled. He leaned over the wall. "I declare this Valley for the kids of Bendale and for the people of Bendale, and as the possible future president of the student council at Bendale Public School, I demand that you stop wrecking the Valley and leave."

The chain saw gurgled and then turned off.

"Should I read the manifesto?" Boris asked me, reaching for his backpack.

"Did you hear someone?" Husky Voice from last night said.

"Nah. Cut it down," Nasal Voice said.

"You're cutting nothing," Boris sang out. He let out a war cry, which I now recognized as his birdcall. "We're never leaving, even if we gotta stay here for a hundred years. Do you hear me? A hundred years!" He began snapping photos with his dad's phone.

"I definitely hear someone," Husky Voice said.

Nasal Voice walked forward and peered up at us. "What are you doing up there?" he said. "Get down before there's trouble."

"We can't come down until you agree to stop what you're doing," Boris said.

"Of all the …" Nasal Voice began to climb up.

Soon we were being glared at by a thin-faced man with bits of stubble around his chin, dark-set eyes and tufts of white hair around his mostly bald head.

Boris held the phone up. "The camera's rolling, and I'm gonna post the video on my Facebook page and I'm tweeting like crazy. We did a television interview last night, and any minute there will be tons of people here protesting. You have no choice but to give up."

"There are two crazy kids in the tree," Nasal Voice called down.

Husky Voice climbed up to join him. He was a large man, with a broad, friendly face. Thick black hair shot out from under his red safety helmet. "Kids, you can't do this. We gotta take this tree down. I know you love to play here, but the City of Bendale sold it to this gentleman, and I got a job to do. So let's talk about it — on the ground."

Husky Voice sounded kind.

"I used to play here when I was your age," he continued. "But we have to make way for the new houses. I have to clear this area out, and unfortunately that means cutting down this tree. I feel bad, boys. I do. But you have to go."

I found myself feeling sorry for him. He did not seem to like his job, at least not now.

Boris fixed his steely-eyed gaze on the two men. "We're not leaving. We're gonna save this tree and the Valley. Soon there will be hundreds of kids here, too, and Sandy will come back, and you'll be on television, and ..."

Nasal Voice huffed and then scowled ominously at Boris's phone. He motioned to Husky Voice and the two men climbed down.

Boris shrugged. "Flavius, can you check if there are any protesters yet?" He handed me the binoculars.

I scrambled up the secondary ladder to the lookout post and raised the binoculars to my eyes. The meadow was empty. I looked to the street. A few cars drove by. None stopped.

"I think the protesters are still having breakfast," I reported.

"Call the cops," Nasal Voice said from the ground. "I want those brats gone in ten minutes ..."

"I think if we promise to leave their tree alone, they'll come down. We can find a way to work around the old trees," Husky Voice said.

"Call the cops!" Nasal Voice thundered. "I don't take orders from children. I own this land now. I've been dealing with delays, disruptions and everyone's 'feelings' about this land, but I've bought it and I'll do what I want. I'll cut down every tree in the Valley if I want. So call the cops."

I didn't hear Husky Voice's reply.

Boris held the phone out for me to see. "I've just posted this to Facebook. What do you think?"

> Wuz up, Bendale? Greetings from the B-Ster. An evil developer is attacking the Valley. We need your help. Come to the Valley. Now. Hurry. If you have a Twitter account, use #RallyInTheValley

"I love it," I said.

Who wouldn't answer such an inspiring call to action?

"It's already working," Boris said. "Someone named @TheValleyMonster has posted a few things — about saving the Valley for the kids at Bendale."

"Who could that be?" I said.

"Doesn't matter. The kids will be here soon. You want a Pop-Tart or a banana muffin?" Boris asked me.

Again, the answer was obvious, and he handed me one of each.

CHAPTER TWELVE

"They've been up there for two hours already," Nasal Voice told the two police officers. "And get that camera out of my face!" he roared at Ernie.

Ernie adjusted the lens for a close-up. Sandy reapplied her lipstick.

"Ruff, ruff, ruff, ruff," the cute mutt barked. He peed on Nasal Voice's shoe.

"Control your dog," Nasal Voice said, jumping back. "That's disgusting."

The woman pulled on the leash. The cute mutt strained against it, raising his leg every so often to try and hit Nasal Voice.

Dogs pee to mark their territory. I'd never seen a dog claiming a person's foot, though.

"That dog's taken quite a liking to Nasal Voice's shoe," I told Boris. "Come look."

Boris was sitting on the floor, his thumbs furiously tapping the phone's screen. "I don't understand it," he fretted. "I'm tweeting every ten minutes, and I must've uploaded a hundred photos to Instagram. No one's commenting or even following me. But @TheValleyMonster has about a thousand likes on his Facebook page and all my pictures are posted on his site, too." He put the phone down.

"And where is everyone? A few adults aren't going to change things."

I looked out in the hope that some Bendale kids were coming. For a moment, I got excited. Four figures were headed our way. My joy turned to intense fear.

"Boris, our parents!"

Boris jumped to his feet.

"Hey, Mom. Hey, Dad. Over here!" he yelled.

"Shhhh," I whispered. "They'll hear you."

"Umm — yeah," Boris said. "That's the point."

"But ... But ..."

For some strange reason, he didn't see the danger. Our parents were here — and we'd snuck out of our houses last night and slept in Roma.

"Hey, guys," Boris said. "I knew you'd come. Isn't it great? Soon we'll have hundreds of protesters. They were going to cut down this tree."

Our parents looked confused.

"Are these your boys?" Nasal Voice said. "You better get them down, right now, or they'll be in huge trouble."

Boris's dad didn't even look at Nasal Voice. "Boys, you didn't tell us what you were doing, you misled us and you slept outside last night," he said. "But I understand why, and if you come down, I promise the punishment will not be that serious. Please listen to reason. I know you love the tree fort, only you can't stay here. They're building houses. They own the land."

"That's right," Nasal Voice said. "And would you please get out of my face with that camera," he told Ernie.

Ernie popped a Tic Tac into his mouth. The camera didn't budge.

"Did you have something for breakfast, Adrian?" my mom asked me. "I could run home and make you a sandwich."

I assured her that we were well stocked with snacks.

"Sorry, Dad," Boris said. "We feel bad about sneaking out. But we knew they were gonna chop this tree down this morning if we didn't do something, so we had to start Operation Rally in the Valley right away."

"Boris, you can't stay in a tree house forever," his dad said. "Come down and we can talk."

A police officer stepped closer. Ernie's camera swung toward him. "Young man, I'm Officer Bracken. I need you both to come down so we can discuss the matter."

"I'm sorry, Officer Bracken, but we can't do that," Boris said.

"Do you mind if I come up, then?" Officer Bracken asked.

"Not at all," Boris said.

Boris held his arm out to me and we shook, Roman-style. It helped, but not enough to stop sheer terror from flooding my senses and paralyzing my mind — and unleashing a very unpleasant desire to visit a washroom — as in right away. I knew a bathroom break would be inconvenient — Boris needed me, and so did the Valley.

I am intimidated by people in authority, totally and completely intimidated, like by teachers and principals and bus drivers and lunchroom monitors and janitors and swim instructors and lifeguards and older kids and crossing guards and hairdressers and firefighters and babysitters and waitstaff and ushers in theaters and salespeople — and definitely police officers.

Boris has hinted that I might consider working on my self-confidence.

Officer Bracken popped his head over the wall. "You are certainly well prepared," he said.

"Thanks, Officer," Boris said. "I shoulda brought more Nutella, though. I mean, one jar? What was I thinking?"

Officer Bracken laughed. "You're right — you can never have enough. Anyway, the gentleman down there has explained to me that his company has the right to clear this land for a building development, so there's not much you can do to stop it. Sorry. He says the City has already decided things."

"Officer Bracken, I know you're doing your job," Boris said, "and we're causing trouble for you, but the Valley is more than a place for kids to play. It's a part of what it means to grow up here. We can't just let someone cut down all the trees and build a bunch of houses. If people knew what was happening, about what the evil developer is trying to do, then they'd join us and we could stop him. I know it. So I'm really sorry, but we can't come down."

Officer Bracken gave us a sideways glance. "I respect what you're trying to do," he said. "I really do. I grew up in this town. Spent I don't know how many hours playing here, tossing the football around or just hanging out." He sighed and looked wistfully toward the meadow. "It's a beautiful place, isn't it? I didn't think the City had actually sold the land yet." He leaned forward. "Can I tell you something? I'm on your side." He winked at us and his head disappeared.

"They won't listen to me," Officer Bracken said to

Nasal Voice. "There's nothing I can do about it without a court order or their parents' permission. Do you have a court order?"

"Of course I don't. How would I have time to get a court order? Do your job and get rid of them," Nasal Voice said. "Haul the spoiled brats down and arrest them."

"Don't you dare," my mother said. "You lay one hand on my Adrian and I'll press charges."

"No one is getting arrested," Officer Bracken said. "I don't even know if technically they're breaking the law. Do you have documentation proving you own this land? Until I see proof of that, I have to consider this public property, which means everyone has the right to be on it. They have the right to protest in a peaceful manner, and they're being peaceful."

Officer Bracken and his partner left.

"*Has* the sale gone through?" Boris's father asked Nasal Voice.

"The sale is all but done," Nasal Voice said to our parents. "I have permission to clear the land so a proper survey can be done. Your kids are costing me a fortune. Did you raise them to be selfish and entitled? They're a menace to society."

"Adrian is a wonderful boy, and we've always taught him to stand up for what he believes in," my mom said.

"Adrian? Is he the dark-haired one or the dumpy one?" Nasal Voice said.

That stung me to the core. I am somewhat sensitive about my appearance.

"How dare you speak about my boy like that!" my mom said.

Everyone began talking at once. Boris pulled out a water gun from a duffel bag and brought the barrel to shoulder height.

"What are you …?" I didn't have time to finish my question.

Nasal Voice wiped the water from his face and jacket. Boris had scored a direct hit.

"Don't talk about my bud like that," Boris called out.

"They're little felons — a pair of … criminals!" Nasal Voice screamed and stormed off.

"Okay, boys," Boris's dad said. "Enough with the water, please." I believe I detected a slight wink from Boris's dad, and possibly I saw Husky Voice smile. It was hard to tell. I was too busy letting out an ancient Roman battle cry. Encouraging signs perhaps, but we were no closer to saving the Valley. Boris tugged on my arm.

"They'll probably leave us alone for a while," Boris said, "and soon we'll have a huge crowd and we'll be busy. You want some lunch?" Boris said.

"I'm a bit peckish," I said.

Boris reached into a garbage bag and pulled out a cereal box and two bowls. "There's milk in that cooler," he said, digging out two spoons from his back pocket.

"I should've brought my Science Fair notebook," I said. "I had some calculations to finish for the new input values for the trains. I might be able to improve velocity by three percent without any increase in energy usage."

Boris tossed me a bag of chips. "That's not a bad idea — the Science Fair, I mean. Not quite sure what you meant by the other stuff. How do you enter?"

"You just give your name to Ms. Crimpet and ..." I pointed to his phone. "Can I use that for a second?"

He handed it to me. I quickly found the Science Fair announcement on the Bendale website. "Take a look," I said, giving the phone back.

THE BENDALE TRIPLE-R SCIENCE-PALOOZA

REDUCE, REUSE, RECYCLE

THE THEME THIS YEAR IS THE ENVIRONMENT.
COME TO THE GYM MONDAY, APRIL 23,
AND SHOW OFF YOUR
SCIENCE-PALOOZA EXHIBIT.
WIN PRIZES
AND HAVE FUN, TOO!

Sponsored by the BENDALE SCIENCE CLUB and
Sheckle, Minx and Associates Real Estate and Insurance Adjusters

Speak to Ms. Crimpet to register

Boris looked at it for a long time. A huge grin spread across his face.

I assumed he saw some kids coming. I stood up.

Nothing.

"I should enter the Science Fair — and maybe get to know the brainiacs a bit better," Boris said.

"Good idea — but you'll have to get right to work. You only have four weeks to finish your exhibit."

"I can worry about that after this operation. So ... can't be much longer until the kids come. I just sent out another tweet." He looked at the phone. "The Valley

Monster's been tweeting about the Valley almost as much as me. This last one is a bit weird: 'I'm trying to save the Valley — Vote for Me!'"

Boris pulled two small speakers from a bag.

"Making another speech?" I asked.

"Nah, setting up the speakers."

"I can see that. I'm wondering why."

He attached a cord from the phone to the speakers and pressed the screen. The music began.

Not a bad idea. Music might make the time pass a bit faster.

Suddenly, without warning, Boris dropped into his squat — and then, as the beat got louder, he began to tap his right foot.

A guitar began to play off the bass, then the saxophone set off into a soulful riff.

Boris is a jazz man above all else, but the blues on his dad's phone suited the mood.

Graceful? He is not.

Nimble? Not that either.

But a Boris Snodbuckle in full dance mode is still a joyful sight, his head held back, arms flailing, feet sliding every which way.

I tried to worry about school and the police and my parents. I did. I resisted with every fiber of my being. Then, I allowed myself the occasional toe tap, followed by a head bob. No harm in that.

The groove got deeper.

I got up, defeated by the rhythm.

Together we danced away the boredom.

CHAPTER THIRTEEN

Boris woke me. That had never happened in our 117 sleepovers. I instantly knew that meant something very foul was afoot. I heard engine noises in the distance and the sound of tree branches crunching, and saw lights getting brighter and brighter. Suddenly, a backhoe broke through the trees and trundled over to Roma. It was a truly terrifying sight, Nasal Voice driving toward us.

"Roma's under attack," Boris said, grabbing his water gun.

The scoundrel had chosen to attack at the moment our numbers were lowest. Once the developer said he was going to his lawyer's office, the crowd had drifted away. Our parents said they would go home for lunch and come back around five. After we had tired of dancing, we had decided to take advantage of the calm to catch up on our sleep. We were on our own.

Nasal Voice leaped out of the backhoe and climbed up. His face was dark red and sweaty. He looked like he'd lost his mind. He tied a chain around some pieces of wood that supported one of the walls.

"You climbed up, and you can climb down," he said. "I'm pulling this ridiculous tree fort apart, stick by stick if I have to."

Boris let fly with his water gun — a direct hit.

Nasal Voice sneezed a few times and wiped his face.

"I've had it with both of you," he sputtered. "I'm tired of dealing with spoiled children who get trophies for participating and always get good grades and have no idea what it means to work a day in their lives."

He began to climb back down. I raced to the chain, but he'd locked it in place. Roma was not built to withstand the pulling power of a backhoe.

"What do we do?" I cried.

Boris sat on the floor, silent and morose. "No one came," he said quietly. "I tweeted a hundred times, updated my Facebook page and posted a million photos to Instagram. We did two television interviews with Sandy and a phone interview with a newspaper. No one cared. They cared more about what the Valley Monster had to say and he wasn't even here. I don't understand what went wrong." Elbows on his knees, he pressed his chin into his hands.

"I'm sure after dinner more people would have come, at least the Green Goblins," I offered. It pained me to see Boris dejected. Perhaps he'd been too ambitious, but if you don't hope, you never find what is beyond your hopes.

Nasal Voice stood up in the backhoe and pulled out an extremely large paintball gun, with two pellet holders slung across his chest. "No one sprays me with water and gets away with it, especially not a pair of brats."

Boris eyed me carefully. That look meant only one thing. The Snodbuckle had come to a decision.

"Run, Flavius!"

We flung ourselves over the far wall and scrambled down using our emergency escape ropes. Splattering paint pellets against trees was all the motivation we needed to run full out.

"You can't escape! You're both getting painted. Head to toe!" Nasal Voice screamed from behind. He began to laugh, a sound akin to a hyena gargling water.

We broke out into the open. Boris pulled me toward Suicide Steep. I risked a quick glance back.

"We should split up," I told Boris. "He can't catch us both. I'll lead him away, and you can get to the bikes."

"No chance, Flavius," Boris said, over his shoulder. "We stick together. Go for the Shortcut to the ravine."

We skirted the bottom of Suicide Steep and headed to the right. Paint pellets flew overhead.

I cringed. The Shortcut was the nickname we'd given to a nasty patch of brambles and thorn bushes. Bendale students would dare each other to walk through it. I'd never been brave enough.

Boris charged full on.

"Ahhhhhhhhhh!" he screamed.

I closed my eyes and followed.

"Ahhhhhhhhhh!" I screamed.

"Ahhhhhhhhhh, you brats!" Nasal Voice screamed.

Boris's quick thinking provided us with a solid sixty-foot lead, with scratches from head to toe a small price to pay. A hill rose before us. Once over that, we could descend into the ravine. I assumed Boris believed the mud and wet and bugs in the ravine would give us a distinct advantage; Boris and I were experienced in filth. Several construction vehicles were lined up at the top of the hill. They stared down at us like sentries on the rampart of a castle.

"Charge, Flavius," Boris roared.

"At your side, Octavius," I sounded.

"Stop …" Nasal Voice gasped. "Stop … you brats." Nasal Voice began coughing violently, his hands on his knees, bent deeply at the waist. His lack of fitness had saved us.

I joined Boris at the top of the hill next to a front-end loader.

"Looks like we're out of danger," I said, watching Nasal Voice wheezing on the ground.

Boris responded glumly. "I thought things would work this time, Adrian, especially after we won the swings back for the primaries. I really thought kids would come. Everyone loves the Valley, don't they?" He shook his head. "But maybe they don't," he said. "I don't really know … I thought we had a real chance to change something, to help. This wasn't just about winning the Green Goblins' votes for me." He shrugged helplessly. "Sorry if I looked like a coward running away. He had the advantage in machinery and fire power."

Boris Snodbuckle lacking courage? I almost laughed out loud. Unfortunately, as for Operation Rally in the Valley, he was correct. We'd failed.

A murmuring of voices caught my attention.

"What the —? Who are —? Where in the —?" Nasal Voice stuttered, lifting his head up.

The famous Snodbuckle grin spread from ear to ear. Boris grabbed my forearm, and I his.

Marching into the Valley were no less than four hundred placard-waving kids and adults chanting, "Valley Monster — cha-cha-cha! Valley Monster — cha-cha-cha!"

Nasal Voice ran toward them, or perhaps *staggered* would be more accurate.

Boris and I followed — and got a serious surprise. Leading them was Robert and his crew, with Michael waving a white sign with blue lettering that read — "Valley Monster."

And then to my absolute, total surprise — and I mean total — I saw Boris's father striding right behind them, and farther back, the inimitable Lynda Skittle, my parents, Boris's mom and Officer Bracken.

Pride, joy, elation and delight.

As always, Boris captured the moment perfectly. He began to do the stir-the-pot dance, singing out, "Go Valley — Go Valley — Go Valley — Go Valley."

Nasal Voice shook a fist at the crowd. "Get off my land or I'll get a court order so fast your heads will spin off your shoulders."

"It's not quite your land," Boris's dad said. "We went to City Hall and found out you *forgot* to do an environmental study required for rezoning, which you need before you can cut the grass, let alone a tree."

Michael held his poster in the air. "He didn't do the study — and that ain't cool with the Valley Monster."

"And you lied to the City and faked a report about how your project wouldn't affect the ravine that runs through the Valley," my mom charged.

"The Valley Monster digs the ravine," Robert crowed.

"And this man told me an even more interesting fact," Officer Bracken said, pointing to Boris's dad. "The Valley isn't parkland, but is protected in a different way. The wise founders of Bendale gave a right of way in the

Valley to the federal government to prevent future city councils from selling the land off quickly and easily. You were allowed to do a survey. That doesn't affect the actual land. But as soon as you begin any construction, you'd have to go to the Municipal Board and apply for an amendment to the original deed ..." The officer laughed. "Bottom line, you can't build here unless the federal government agrees. So tell me, did the feds give you permission?"

"The feds don't really care about this place," Nasal Voice said with disgust.

"Did you apply to amend the deed and get the feds' permission?" the officer pressed.

Nasal Voice waved him off. "You know I didn't."

"You have no respect for the law," Robert said gleefully. "The Valley Monster don't dig that."

"And you're mean and I bet your feet smell," Lynda said.

"Bendale students aren't gonna let you get away with this," Robert said, striding forward. "The Valley Monster loves the Valley too much for that."

Michael waved his Valley Monster poster.

I had a horrible feeling Michael was winking at me.

"The Valley Monster is here to stop you," Robert said to Nasal Voice, "and there's no way you can win, not with the entire school behind me."

"No way," Michael said.

"Valley Monster, cha-cha-cha!" Wong, Henson and Daniels chanted.

Nasal Voice snorted and glared at the crowd. "I would've gotten away with it if it hadn't been for —"

"Three cheers for the Valley Monster," Michael cried.

Robert held his arms over his head. Wong, Henson and Daniels let out a roar and began to chant. Soon the crowd joined in, with Robert and Michael clapping along. Nasal Voice stomped off.

"Valley Monster," Robert cried.

"Cha-cha-cha," his crew answered.

"Valley Monster," Robert repeated.

This time the entire crowd joined in.

"Cha-cha-cha," they roared in unison.

It was a bittersweet moment for me. Robert had again managed to take credit for Boris's ideas and good work. But the Valley had been saved — our dear, beloved Valley would not fall under the deadly kiss of the chain saw and the front-end loader. I was torn between elation and frustration.

Boris did not, evidently, feel the same.

"We did it," he cried over and over, clapping to the beat as the crowd answered Robert with another "cha-cha-cha."

How could I stay angry about Robert in the presence of a joyful Snodbuckle?

I suppose we had done it, and not just us. Boris's father had found out about the environmental study and the federal government, my mother had determined that Nasal Voice had lied about the ravine and, while it hurts to admit it, Robert deserved some credit for bringing all those kids to the Valley.

Along with Boris, I cha-cha-cha'd away with the rest of the crowd.

PART IV

Operation Broadway

CHAPTER FOURTEEN

The sting of seeing Brandon, president of the Green Goblins, present Robert with the Organic Golden Hemp Award for saving the Valley at yesterday's school assembly had not yet worn off — not for me, anyway. We still had ten minutes before school started, and feeling somewhat antisocial, I suggested we hang out by ourselves underneath the big maple tree by the parking lot.

"I'd love to," Boris said, "but I gotta check in with Mrs. Brundleford every day this week. She made me promise to come on time every day from now to the end of the year. She said I have to be responsible."

Mrs. Brundleford was the school administrator, and she ran the office. I brushed aside my disappointment and agreed to join him.

"Thanks for checking in," Mrs. Brundleford said when she saw us. "You're a little early."

"It's because I need to speak to the Principal," Boris said. "We're here on business."

"What kind of business? I'm not sure this is a good time," Mrs. Brundleford said, wide-eyed.

"School business," Boris said, laughing heartily. "I'll let myself in."

"He's very busy," she said, her voice rising.

"I know," Boris said. He turned the knob and pushed the door open.

Mrs. Brundleford jumped to her feet and scurried over.

"I'm sorry, sir. He said it was school business," she said to the Principal.

"What happened?" the Principal said, sounding alarmed.

Boris laughed again. "You guys are funny today," he said. "I have to check in before school, remember?"

The Principal closed his eyes slightly, and his head jerked back. "You're actually doing it?"

"Clear-cut case of Rule One," Boris said. "Don't break school rules, unless there's a really good reason."

"Clear-cut," I said.

The Principal blinked at Boris, his face expressionless and somewhat pale. He placed a piece of paper on his desk. It looked like a poster. His right eye narrowed. "Okay. Thanks, Boris. I'm hoping we can get through one day without your being sent to my office. What do you think?"

"I don't think that will be a problem," Boris said.

"Actually, the odds are almost one hundred percent he'll be sent to the office today," I said.

"Huh?" the Principal said.

"Boris is sent to the office an average of four times a week. He didn't get sent here yesterday, so the odds are he'll be back," I explained. "It's simple math."

"So I'll see you later, then," Boris said.

The Principal's left eye narrowed.

"Before I go, though, I wanted to show you my list of goals if I'm elected president of the student council." Boris pulled a sheet of paper from his pocket.

"Can I take a look?" I asked.

"Sure."

I quickly scanned the list.

If he did half these things, Boris would be a legend — or rather, even more of a legend.

1. Kids should vote on what they want to do in gym class — you shouldn't have to play dodgeball every day if you don't want to.
2. Intramural sports will be held at lunch and after school.
3. Grades 1 to 3 get to choose their seats in the lunchroom first.
4. Running is permitted on school property.
5. Wedgies are hereby outlawed.
6. Outdoor recess will happen — rain or shine.
7. Students have the right to appeal detentions.
8. Choir will restart, and money from the Fall Fair will be used to buy instruments.
9. Once a month Bendale students will do something good for the community.

I was impressed, particularly by number 1. I gave the list to the Principal.

"I'll pick it up later," Boris said to him, "when I get sent down."

The Principal grunted.

"See ya," Boris said cheerfully.

The Principal grunted again.

Robert and Michael were waiting outside the Principal's office as we left.

"How's your farting problem?" Robert said to Boris.

"I see you are as funny as usual," I snapped.

"Ignore him," Boris said. He pulled me away. "Take

a look at this," he said to me as we walked down the hallway. He handed me a poster.

Robert and Michael went into the Principal's office.

"Is this from the Principal's desk?" I asked.

"Of course. I'll bring it back when I get sent down," Boris said. "But listen. This is awesome news. I've been thinking of how I can prove myself to the artsy kids. Since I sorta dropped the ball with the little kids and the nature lovers, I've been feeling the pressure." He shook the poster. "And now I think I've got it figured out." He unrolled it.

THE BENDALE DRAMATIC ARTS DEPARTMENT PROUDLY ANNOUNCES

AUDITIONS

FOR A PRODUCTION OF

THE LION KING

Please prepare a song.
Auditions will be held after school this Thursday at 4:00 p.m. in the gym.

MR. FRANKLIN HURLEY
ARTISTIC DIRECTOR

Founder of the Bendale Public School Arts Foundation
President of the Friends of Shakespeare Society
Artistic Director of the Bendale Community Theater
Founding Member of the Hurley Burlies Improv Group
Finalist in the Dare-to-Dream Bendale Talent Night
Co-producer and Star of *Do You Want a Banana with Your Fries?*
— Bendale Fringe Festival

Ms. Crimpet
Second Assistant

"Things are gonna get crazy busy pretty soon with memorizing my lines for Simba and running for president; I might even have to miss Saturday morning cartoons." Boris looked up to the ceiling.

How much can one be expected to sacrifice?

"You should try out, too," Boris said. "It'll be fun to hang out together backstage."

"I — I don't think ... I can't try out."

"You gotta. I've never been in a play, and you know everything about Broadway shows," Boris said.

Broadway was a hobby, and I'd memorized the words to the songs of about twenty-four of Broadway's biggest hits — not that I was counting.

I couldn't be in a real play, though.

"I — I — I don't know what to sing at the audtion," I stammered.

"Neither do I," Boris said. "So what? We'll just go for it. Meet me in the War Room after school and we'll pick out our songs and practice." He threw in the Snodbuckle shuffle, his face aglow with excitement. "Things are coming together, bud," Boris said. "It's too bad about the little kids and the Green Goblins; looks like Robert snookered me there. But once we get our parts, we'll be in tight with the artsy crowd."

"I doubt I'll get a talking part," I said. "On the other hand, 'There's no such thing as a small part.'"

"Huh?" Boris said.

"It's the Golden Rule of the Theater: every actor is important to the show, not just the stars."

Boris put his arm across my shoulders. "I like it," he said. "Not everyone can be Simba. And when I perform on that stage, I'll have as much respect for Robert playing a hyena or Michael playing a cactus as I will for whoever plays Scar or Nala."

"Well said."

"I've got the Science Fair coming up, and if I can do okay there, maybe I can connect with the brainiacs — then all we gotta do is figure out something to sway the popular kids — and, well, there's still hope. Not sure how I'm gonna get them on my side, but we got lots of time to figure that out."

Perhaps Boris was being a tad optimistic. I'd carried out some interviews last recess to determine if Boris was gaining support for his run for president. According to my figures, I had Robert winning by a margin of 98 percent.

The good news was that there was room for improvement.

"What do you think Robert and Michael wanted to talk to the Principal about?" I said.

"Got me," Boris said.

I looked at my watch. "We really need to get to our line. We'll get detention if we're late again."

"We already have detention all this week," Boris said, "so there's nothing to worry about. Let's take a tumble down the hill. Operation Broadway can wait a few minutes."

I followed Boris out the side door to the field.

CHAPTER FIFTEEN

Mr. Sun, Sun, Mr. Golden Sun …
Please shine down on …
Please shine down on …
Please shine down on meeeeee

"That will do," Mr. Hurley said.

Please shine down on …
Please shine down on …

"I said that will do!" Mr. Hurley repeated very loudly.

Stevie Bishop bowed deeply. I wondered which his voice resembled more — a rooster with a sore throat or a dentist's drill.

"Thanks, Stevie. That was … terrific," Ms. Crimpet said. "I'm glad you've decided to get involved with the play."

Mr. Hurley was red-faced. He'd announced before the tryouts that people shouldn't sing too loudly. He had to concentrate on his writing. Apparently, Genghis Khan and Flipity-Dipity were about to play a spirited game of cricket.

"I asked for you to keep it down," Mr. Hurley said. He looked down at his red notebook and began to hum, then sing:

Cricket, Ricket, Ticket, Tosh, I had a doggie
and his name was Bosh.

He put his red notebook down. "I can't believe I have to direct *The Lion King*. I mean — please! Me? Directing *The Lion King*? When I had my own original play ready to go?" He gripped his hair and pulled — hard. I thought I detected a tear in his eye. "It would have been magnificent. What was the Principal thinking? Last year's play was such a huge hit. The reviews were … magnificent."

I had attended the premiere of that production. It was called *I'm Depressed, I'm Sad, I'm Lonely — So Let's Sing About It*. I'd heard rumors that several parents complained to the Principal and demanded that this year Mr. Hurley do something more cheerful — and maybe written by someone else. The eighth graders were boycotting Mr. Hurley and were refusing to participate in the play at all.

I glanced at the door. Boris had not arrived yet, and I was getting worried. Our detention had ended an hour ago.

"Can we have Frieda Bowman next," Ms. Crumpet said quietly.

"Just keep it down," Mr. Hurley said, snatching his red notebook.

"My name is Frieda. I'm going to sing 'Edelweiss' from *The Sound of Music*."

I began to have trouble swallowing, and I also experienced a sick sensation in the pit of my stomach. My love for Frieda had begun the first day of first grade after Michael Beverley broke my favorite pencil and called me poopy pants. Now, I realize that his name-calling was merely a cover for his own insecurities, but I was a sensitive child back then and took his harsh words to heart. I had been pouting at my desk, fighting back tears, when I felt a fist punch me in the back. I turned and saw Frieda for the first time, a dazzling beauty with long, straight brown hair and bangs cropped with mathematical precision, an oval face and pudgy cheeks and the most magnetic brown eyes.

"Stop sniffing," she said. "It's gross." She looked me over. "Are you crying?"

I showed her my broken pencil.

"Don't be a baby. You should bring extras." She pulled a yellow pencil with an H2 tip from her case and gave it to me.

"Thank you," I said. "What's your name?"

"Frieda."

"I'm Adrian."

She went back to reading her book, but from that moment we were bonded, at least I to her. And I knew I would be forever. It remains unfortunate that Frieda does not share the same passionate feelings for me — or more accurately, any feelings.

I closed my eyes and waited.

Angelic. Awe-inspiring. Miraculous.

Her voice was like heaven's choir, her tone soft and melodic. Lost and befuddled, I let myself drift off, captivated. Frieda bowed and took her seat.

"That was wonderful," Ms. Crimpet said. "A lovely rendition."

Mr. Hurley pulled at his hair and chewed his pen, and then wrote something in his red notebook. Ms. Crimpet gave him a sharp glance, and I thought she looked irritated about something. She called out, "Can we have Michael Beverley, please."

I admit I desperately wished Michael Beverley would sing badly, even horribly. Unfortunately, he sang with the easy confidence of a professional, in perfect pitch, and in a wistful tone that rang clear as a bell.

When he finished, the door at the back of the gym opened. Boris and two men carrying a trumpet and a saxophone, respectively, walked toward Mr. Hurley. Behind them another man with a double bass struggled to keep up.

"Excuse me, Mr. Hurley," Boris said.

Mr. Hurley let out a huff and ripped a piece of paper from his red notebook, crumpled it and heaved it at a garbage can. The ball of paper bounced off the wall, rolled along the floor and ended up under the piano.

Mr. Hurley began to sing:

We hit the ball, we swing the bat,
We eat some Danish and we all get fat …

"Mr. Hurley?" Boris repeated.

Mr. Hurley slammed the table. "You made me lose my train of thought. Do you understand what you've done? That's genius lost forever."

Ms. Crimpet rolled her eyes. "What is it, Boris?" she said.

"Sorry I'm late," Boris said. "Had to round up the band. We'll just hang out on the side until it's my turn."

"Your band?" Mr. Hurley said. "Where'd you …?"

"I like to catch Jazz Sundays at the Rex Hotel," Boris said. "I asked the boys if they could help me out."

"No problem, B-Ster," the trumpeter said. "Always ready to kick it with a Snodbuckle."

"Any chance you could play for the other kids?" Ms. Crimpet asked.

"I can't concentrate if ..." Mr. Hurley whimpered.

"That would be cool," the trumpeter said. "Should we set up on the stage?"

"Yes, anywhere you like," Ms. Crimpet said.

"Should I go on now?" Boris said.

Mr. Hurley looked up. "What's a good rhyme for Penelope?" he said.

"Catastrophe?" Boris said.

Mr. Hurley crossed something out with his pen and began to write furiously in his red notebook.

"Go ahead, Boris," Ms. Crimpet said.

The band got ready.

"And a one, and a two, and a one-two-three-four," Boris called.

The trio began.

Boris had wrestled with his song choice, unable to decide between "Bohemian Rhapsody" by Queen and "Mack the Knife," which was my suggestion.

As soon as he held out his arms and closed them to imitate a shark bite, I knew he had opted for the latter. Jazz is Boris's sweet spot. No surprise that he was nailing "Mack the Knife." His stage presence, theatricality, energy and sense of humor made it a mesmerizing performance, right down to the dramatic ending where he got down on one knee and let loose with a few dozen arm shark bites.

The room went dead quiet.

Simba was his.

I'd never been more proud to be Boris's sidekick.

Boris bowed, first to the audience and then to the band. The band bowed back.

Peals of laughter echoed off the walls and rose louder and louder.

Mr. Hurley threw his pen down. "That's the last straw. I can't work with this mayhem. Ms. Crimpet, you'll have to finish the auditions. Meet me in my office afterward and I'll make the final decisions."

He snatched his red notebook and began to hum a tune.

There was something something something for Penelope ...

and her something something something was a catastrophe.

"Pure magic," he declared, and then left, with his fist shaking, thrust high overhead.

Ms. Crimpet's upper lip turned up for an instant. "Thanks, Boris. That was terrific. I liked the shark bites, too. Can I have Adrian Nickels next?"

It's one thing to sing the entire musical score of *Les Misérables* in the privacy of your own bedroom, and another to perform in front of a real audience. My throat instantly lost whatever moisture it had, as if I'd drunk a glass of sand. I considered it a tremendous piece of bad luck. On unsteady legs, I made my way to the stage.

As I passed Michael, he said loudly enough for all to hear, "Ten bucks says he sounds like a duck."

"Twenty bucks says he wets his pants," Robert said.

That comment had a viral comedy effect. Michael was unable to sit in his chair. He ended up lying on the floor, presumably so he could laugh harder. Jessica and Cinny were doubled over. Jonah and Stevie, ever ready to join in on a chance to laugh at others, high-fived. I worried my legs would not support my weight.

Boris put his arm around my shoulders and pulled me toward the stage.

"How'd you like it? Was the ending too much?" he said to me.

"It was perfect," I said. "It showed off your triple-threat talent."

Boris shrugged. "You picked the perfect song for me, Adrian. The rest was easy. But do you think Mr. Hurley liked it?"

"I'm sure. He was writing in his red notebook the entire time."

Boris let his breath out. "Thanks, Adrian. You're the best. I was a bit worried. I haven't sung a lot in public, not like this anyway. So what are you singing?"

" 'If I Were a Rich Man' from *Fiddler on the Roof*."

"Can you guys handle 'If I Were a Rich Man'?" Boris asked the band.

The trumpeter nodded. "We'll do it in the key of C," he said.

"Just pretend you're singing to Frieda," Boris whispered.

I forced my breathing under control, and let myself imagine Frieda and me at the Burger Pit sharing a banana-mango milkshake — with one straw.

The trio played softly at first, and I, taking their cue,

sang likewise, focusing first on the right pitch, building in tone and volume as the song progressed. The crowd grew quiet — tired of laughing at me, no doubt. Halfway through, I ceased to notice them. The lyrics, the rhythms and most of all the vision of Frieda and me, together at last, transported me to another place.

I didn't remember the song ending. It finished on its own somehow.

Boris was on his feet, clapping and whistling. Then a curious thing happened. The other students began clapping as well. Of course, I knew they were mocking me. I thanked the band and left the stage.

"That was very good, Adrian, excellent. I really liked it," Ms. Crimpet said. "Jessica is next."

Ms. Crimpet is a kind woman, and I appreciated her pretending to like my song. I took a seat next to Boris.

"Hey, Buck Breath," Robert hissed. "Way to make an even bigger doofus of yourself today than you did at the swings when you hung upside down like a fat bat."

Boris paid no heed.

"You really are a freak," Robert said. "And guess what? I'm gonna kick your buckle butt in the election."

"You're a freak, too," Michael said to me.

Jessica's song interrupted their fun. She wore a white wig and a dress made out of duct tape and playing cards.

I braced myself as the opening line from "Poker Face" rang out.

Granted, it was a classic Lady Gaga number and she nailed the dress, but I found her singing flat and offbeat. The audience clapped and cheered her on.

There truly is no business like show business.

CHAPTER SIXTEEN

Boris rested one foot on Gordie and leaned an arm against the fence. We'd been collecting materials all recess to build the all-time largest inukshuk, which is an Inuit art form where you pile rocks in the shape of a person. We'd piled the rocks in the corner of the field.

"Hey, Snod Pod!"

Lynda Skittle stood before us, hands on hips. She wore a red cotton dress that extended a little below her knees, green and gray leggings and a straw sun hat. Her sidekick, Maggie, waved at me.

Boris reached into his backpack. "You want a granola bar?" he said.

He gave them one each.

"You still running for president?" Lynda asked sharply, chomping into her snack.

Boris's eyes twinkled. I could tell he liked her. "I am," he said.

"You know anything 'bout a wedgie that happened yesterday?" she asked. "Tommy says he got pulled."

Boris and I replied that we had no information regarding that incident.

"It's getting worse — not better," she said, adding a tremendous foot stomp. Her eyes blazed. "Your hair's not great — but we're getting pulled to death out there, and Robert's not stopping it like he promised!"

She glared at Boris and me, as if daring us to disagree.

"If I'm lucky enough to be president of the student council, I want to appoint anti-bullying representatives in each grade. So if you're having problems, like getting pulled, you don't have to go to a teacher, which can cause more trouble, but you tell your rep. The rep tells student council, and we'll work with the Principal and teachers to deal with it," Boris said.

"That's a lot of words," Lynda said.

"I suppose," Boris said gently.

I made a mental note to write a catchy sound bite to express Boris's anti-bullying idea.

Lynda screwed up her eyes and stared at the top of Boris's head. "What's wrong with your hair?" she said.

Boris patted his hair down. We'd met early this morning to work on the campaign, and Boris perhaps needed a few more minutes to work his flow.

"Robert uses gel, and he looks like a president," Lynda said.

"His hair is awesome," Maggie declared.

"Let's go, Maggs," Lynda said abruptly.

The pair left. Maggie turned and waved at us.

It turned out to be an open house, of sorts. Robert and Michael came over.

"Congrats on the award," Boris said. "It looked bad for the Valley until you guys showed up. How awesome is it that the developer can't build houses."

Robert smirked. "No big deal. Just trying to help."

And the visitors kept coming.

Brandon, president of the Green Goblins, sidled over.

"Hi, guys," he offered. He looked down at the ground.

Robert rolled his eyes and Michael began giggling uncontrollably.

Boris and I said hello.

"Hey, Robert," Brandon said. "I was speaking with the other members of the Green Goblins, and since I'm sorta the president of the club, they asked me to ask you, or at least to invite you, or at least ... anyway ... to ask you if you wanted to ... come to our next meeting — and I know it's up to you, of course — and you could see if you maybe kinda wanted to join, since you obviously love the environment and you won the Organic Golden Hemp Award and —" He stopped short.

Robert and Michael had burst out laughing. Brandon's cheeks were a fiery red.

"We'll join," Boris said.

"Sorry," Brandon said, no louder than a whisper. "The Principal told us that would be impossible, and with the Styrofoam cup thing ... I know you want to help, but ..."

Boris's shoulders drooped. "Yeah. I get it. No worries."

Brandon turned to leave.

"Hey, don't go. I wanna hear more about the Green Goblins," Robert said.

"How many members you got?" Michael said.

"Eight," Brandon said brightly.

They burst out laughing again. Brandon cast a depressed look our way — and left. He was met by Lynda and Maggie, and the three of them walked back toward the school entrance together. Lynda was gesturing wildly with her hands. That kid sure seemed to have a lot to say.

Robert collected himself and with a nod of his head said, "Hey, B-Ster. How's the campaign going?"

I was immediately on my guard. Robert never used Boris's real nickname.

"Pretty good," Boris said, in his customary good-natured way. Unlike me, he does not let their mean-spirited insults affect him too much. "It's been hard to get people to listen to my ideas, maybe. How are things going with you?"

"Very awesome," he said. "I decided to put out a campaign poster — with a list of my ideas. You should do it, too. We put them up all over the school, me and my friends, so it didn't take long."

"We had half the school helping," Michael said.

Robert chuckled. "Nice of people to do it, don't you think?"

Boris and I agreed.

"Here's a copy." Robert pulled a paper out of his pocket. "What do you think?"

Boris read it quickly and then gave it to me.

I was flabbergasted. "These are Boris's ideas. Every last one. How did you ...?"

Robert held his arms out. "So weird. Really? Coincidence — or what?"

"Total weirdness," Michael said.

"I've already put the posters up — all over school — so ..." Robert shrugged. "You'll just need to get some new ideas. No big deal. Right?"

"I guess ..." Boris stared at the paper.

"Hey," Robert said brightly. "I almost forgot to tell you that Hurley posted the roles for *The Lion King* on the main bulletin board. You should check it out. You might be happy if you do."

"Totally happy," Michael said.

I forced myself not to leap in the air and click my heels.

"Did either of you get a part?" Boris asked.

"We did," Robert said, "but not as important as yours."

"There's no such thing as a small part," Boris said.

"Huh?" Michael said.

"The Golden Rule of the Theater: everyone involved in the show is important, from the stars to the people who don't even have a line," Boris said.

"I totally agree, B-Ster," Robert said. "Golden Rule all the way."

"For sure," Michael said. "The Golden Rule is totally cool, especially the part about the guy who doesn't even have a line. That dude is a superstar."

"Let's go check it out," Boris said to me.

"Good idea," Robert said. "We'll come, too. I wanna check it out ... again."

"I just gotta chain Gordie up," Boris said.

Robert flashed his white toothy grin. "We'll meet you there."

Boris and I chained Gordie and doubled back. I held on to a tiny spark of hope that I'd gotten a role, however minor. I knew that was highly unlikely and had decided to help with lighting or set design, or whatever else Mr. Hurley needed me to do.

A large crowd had gathered by the bulletin board, and we had to wait to get close enough to read the posting.

"Were they joking?" Boris said to me.

"You're the only joke here, Snot-Buckle," Robert said.

He and Michael broke out into hysterics, with Wong, Henson and Daniels providing the backup chuckles.

I immediately saw the joke. Stevie had been given the role of the Young Simba.

"There must be a mistake," I said to Boris. "Stevie can't meet the musical demands of Young Simba." Boris didn't answer. "Young Simba has to carry the first half of the play," I continued. "This can't be true. What's Mr. Hurley thinking?"

"So tell me," Michael said to Robert. "I understand that the Golden Rule of the Theater means there's no such thing as a small part. Is a rock a small part?"

He and his cronies lost their minds laughing at that. I couldn't understand them sometimes. I went back to searching for Boris's name. Michael had been given the starring role of Simba the Elder. I silently cursed his silky smooth voice. Frieda had been justly rewarded for her magnificent performance with the nod for Nala. Scar went to Brandon. His singing had a surprisingly dark edge, so I agreed with that. Henson got Mufasa. Perhaps a stretch, but I could live with it. More difficult to accept was Robert as Rafiki, the mystic monkey, which smacked of a popularity contest. Jessica was Simba's mom. Jonah was Pumbaa, the warthog; he was somewhat short and squat, so perhaps.

Then I saw it.

Adrian Nickels: Timon

Timon, the fast-talking, wisecracking meerkat, the comic glue of the entire production, it was a dream come true. I would be singing "The Lion Sleeps Tonight," also known by the chorus "Wimoweh," a classic originally written in 1939 by Solomon Linda and the Evening Birds, and made famous in the 1950s by the Weavers. Sidekick to a star in real life, I would be a sidekick on stage as well.

"No small parts," Boris murmured.

Carried away by the prospect of playing Timon, I realized I had not found Boris's name. I scanned lower on the page.

Boris Snodbuckle: Rock No. 2

"We should get to class," Boris said, turning away.

My head spun. How could Mr. Hurley have made such a remarkably bad decision? Stevie couldn't sing, and he didn't have the Snodbuckle acting chops. Young Simba was Boris's role. Had to be.

"There goes Mr. Rock. Is he the star of the show?" Michael said to Robert.

"No. He's just a rock. I just hope Snodsickle doesn't wreck the play like he wrecks everything else," Robert mocked.

Boris had taught me his steely-eyed stare, and I used it as I passed by them. Inside, I was a cauldron of emotion. This was a disaster of epic proportions, and after Boris's fantastic audition, it was the last thing I expected.

The sweet taste of being cast as Timon had turned sour.

CHAPTER SEVENTEEN

Ms. Crimpet tinkled the piano keys. Stevie and Jonah threw Sour Gummi Bears at each other. Jessica complained to Cinny that she should have been Nala. All the while, his script to the side, no longer needed, Boris silently mouthed Simba's lines. Boris's features exhibited the quiet determination of the Snodbuckle in major study mode. He'd refused to quit, despite the humiliation of countless insults from Robert and his crew. In the two weeks since finding out he was Rock No. 2, Boris had worked tirelessly to learn the Simba role, in case Stevie or Michael quit. He'd also learned Pumbaa's lines by practicing with me. He did a good Pumbaa, capturing the lovable warthog's sense of humor while at the same time maintaining the moral dignity so important to the role.

My work with Jonah was not going well. He found it unbelievably funny that Pumbaa farts, and he would fake them as often as possible.

We were waiting for Mr. Hurley to make a rare appearance at rehearsal when I heard a familiar voice.

"Hey, Golden Rule, you practicing your word?"

Michael sat down beside Boris. Michael said this about fifty times a day.

Unfortunately, the Golden Rule nickname had spread like wildfire. Boris brushed it aside, joking that at least it wasn't related to his last name. I found it cruel, and

I bristled every time I heard it. Boris didn't write the script, and it wasn't his fault that Rock No. 2 said "ouch" when a zebra stepped on him. Otherwise, Rock No. 2 was silent.

Granted, rocks can't talk, but neither can lions.

Stevie whacked Jonah on the butt with a rolled-up script.

"Totally got you, loser," Stevie said.

"Totally didn't," Jonah said.

"Totally did."

"Totally didn't. You don't know nothing," Jonah said.

"I know you're a doofus warthog," Stevie cackled. "Lamest part in the show."

"Uh-uh. What about Rock Number Two?"

"Okay, second lamest."

Stevie then whacked Jonah on the head with his script and took off, with Jonah in hot pursuit.

"This play will be a disaster," Frieda huffed.

I hadn't noticed her take a seat beside me.

"The cast seems rather distracted," I offered.

"They're out of control," she said. "Sometimes I wonder if there's one normal kid in school. And if Jessica and Cinny don't stop chirping me about my role, I'll lose it."

"That must be difficult," I said. My heart was beating violently, and I felt a slight dampness on my forehead and in my armpits. I gathered what was left of my rapidly vanishing courage. "You shouldn't listen to them. Your audition was amazing — a perfect choice of song — suited your lyrical qualities. You were the natural choice for Nala, and I think you're doing wonderful things with the role."

She looked directly at me, which does not happen

often — actually, only four-and-a-half times in my lifetime — and provided me a rare chance to admire her beauty up close.

"Thanks. And you'll be good in ... You're Timon, right?" she asked.

"Yes, Timon, the playmate of the lovable Pumbaa and the —"

"Hurley's a joke," she said, cutting me off. "He doesn't care about this play one bit. He's all about that red notebook and that idiotic Genghis Bunny Ears musical."

"I believe the title is —"

"Stevie's terrible," she continued. "I'd rather have that Boris guy as Simba than Stevie, and so would everyone else. Boris can sing — and at least he remembers his word."

I assumed she was being complimentary — hard to tell. I agreed with her that Boris's timing with his "ouch" was impeccable.

"Everyone knows Hurley's wife and Robert's mom are best friends," she growled, "and that's why he got Rafiki. Life's about who you know."

Mr. Hurley came in. Frieda picked up her science textbook and started reading.

I hadn't had such a long chat with Frieda since Boris and I got our heads stuck in her cubby in fourth grade. We were testing the strength of crazy glue. My romantic life was most definitely looking up.

"Hold it down, hold it down. Let's not destroy the room," Mr. Hurley said. "Why can't you practice your lines instead of yelling at the top of your lungs because I'm a minute late?"

In fact, he was sixteen minutes late.

"This is crunch time, people," Mr. Hurley said. "I have to finish the first draft of my play by the end of the week. I have dozens of producers literally chomping at the bit to see it." He laid his red notebook down carefully and sighed.

"But this play is in trouble. I'm going to have to save the day — as usual. You all need a crash course in acting, in singing, in commanding the attention of an audience and how to captivate them with your stage presence, how to ..." He looked around the class. "I don't expect talent or — let's just say it — my charisma. But I do expect you to take this opportunity to learn from me. So please, pay attention to what you are about to see. It just might change your life."

Mr. Hurley turned his back to us and then without warning whirled around, arms out to his sides, his mouth twisted in a mournful pout.

I confess I hadn't expected him to sing.

Oh Flipity, my Flipity, where oh where can I find her — find her,

Is life a flock of silly birds, flying so silly — Oh silly birds, how you fly — so silly,

Or is life a duck, with feathers, so ducky — Hey there, sweet ducky — how you fly — so ducky ...

Before we could find out what else life was like, a tightly rolled script sailed through the air and struck Mr. Hurley in the chest.

Mr. Hurley's eyes bugged out and his neck bulged.

"Outrageous. This is an attack against the arts, against

drama, against beauty — against ..." He pondered for a moment. "Against the essence of life itself!"

His face was beet red.

"Now, who threw it? I demand to know this instant. It didn't throw itself."

That was certainly true, but no one stepped forward to accept responsibility. I was in shock myself. Who would do such a thing?

Mr. Hurley picked up the script. "Boris Snodbuckle, can you explain to me, to the rest of the cast and to a little thing I call the *magic* of the *theater* why a script with your name written on it hit me in the chest? Can you?"

One look at Boris's face assured me that the accusation was absolutely, completely, unquestionably, totally, certainly and utterly without merit. It was wrong, short and simple. Boris was innocent. I felt better immediately. Mr. Hurley would see that he was wrong and apologize.

"I didn't throw it, Mr. Hurley," Boris said.

"I believe I hold in my hands a script with your name on it!" he screeched. "YOUR NAME! Do you know who I am? You are looking at a man who directed himself in that whimsical one-man show *Do You Want a Banana with Your Fries?* at the Bendale Fringe Festival. I'm the founder of the Bendale Public School Arts Foundation, the Artistic Director of the Bendale Community Theater, a member of the legendary improv troupe the Hurley Burlies. You're lucky to have a professional, instead of a know-nothing English teacher who thinks she's some sort of actor just because she acted on Broadway a few times and did a few movies and TV and now wants to teach because she has so much money she doesn't have to act anymore and ..."

Mr. Hurley took a deep breath to collect himself. "What's your part, Snodbuckle?"

I braced myself.

"Rock Number Two," Boris said.

"Do you have any lines?"

"Not really," Boris said. "I sorta have one line ... or one word, really."

"What is it?"

The cast had divided itself into two groups. There were those who were laughing at Boris — and there was me. Frieda was still reading her book, so I didn't know which group she fell into. I secretly hoped mine.

"'Ouch.' I say it to Zebra Number Two," Boris said when the laughter had died down.

"Correction!" Mr Hurley declared, his chest puffed out, a finger raised in the air. "You used to say 'ouch' to Zebra Number Two. Those days are over. You have lost the privilege. From this point on, Rock Number Two is silent. Do you hear me? Silent!"

Words escaped me. I sat in silence — a tribute to Rock No. 2's lost "ouch."

I felt my love for theater crushed by the injustice of Mr. Hurley's unjust decision.

"You must apologize to the rest of the class, Snodbuckle. They were about to enjoy the unique privilege of seeing me perform, and now that moment is gone. I can't do it. I'm too upset." He crossed his arms. "Mr. Snodbuckle, an apology."

"But I didn't do it," Boris whispered.

"Poor baby," Robert said.

"Snodsy-Podsy's gonna cry," Michael said.

"I don't believe Boris would do such a thing," Ms. Crimpet interjected.

"Mr. Snodbuckle," Mr. Hurley said, in a raised voice, "if you don't apologize this instant, you're out of this production and —"

"Sorry," Boris said, barely loud enough to be heard.

"A little more clearly, please," Mr. Hurley said.

I wanted to disappear from this school — forever. This was awful.

"I'm sorry," Boris said.

"Good. You should be," Mr. Hurley snapped. "Okay, Ms. Crimpet told me you've been working on the opening number. We have thirty minutes left — but I have to leave early — so let's run through it once."

An elbow dug into my ribs.

"What just happened?" Frieda said.

"Oh, um, someone threw a script at Mr. Hurley while he was singing ..."

"Good," Frieda muttered. "He sings like a frog — who can't sing — and had his throat removed — and is dead."

"Um ... Well, the script had Boris's name on it. I guess it was his script. But he didn't throw it," I said heatedly.

"Of course he didn't," Frieda said.

"How do you know?" I gasped.

"Seriously?" she said.

I was unsure how to answer.

"Why are you staring at me like that?" she said.

"I'm ... not sure. No one knows who threw it, but Mr.

Hurley thinks it was Boris and took his 'ouch' away and almost kicked him out of the play," I said.

She rolled her eyes at me. "It's so obvious."

"What is?"

"Who wants to make Boris look bad? Who was sitting close enough to him to steal his script? Who has a good throwing arm? Who's so popular that he can do what he wants and no one will tell on him?"

I felt the veil of stupidity fall from my eyes.

It was obvious.

Michael was sitting next to Boris. He took the script.

And only one person in this room wanted Boris to look bad, had a good throwing arm and was so popular no one would dare tell on him — Robert Pinsent.

"So tell Hurley and get your friend off the hook," Frieda said.

I could only be thankful I hadn't had a big lunch. Otherwise, I would've thrown up.

"Rule Five," I croaked. "I can't do it."

"What does that even mean?" she said.

"One, two, three," Mr. Hurley called out before I could explain.

Thin, shrill voices responded. Mr. Hurley conducted with a blackboard eraser in his right hand.

"Hold it. Hold it," Mr. Hurley yelled.

Stevie hit Jonah with his script.

"Stop!" Mr. Hurley thundered.

Most stopped singing.

"Can we try singing in time to the music?" Mr. Hurley wailed.

Evidently, we could not.

CHAPTER EIGHTEEN

It was opening night, and a packed house of parents and friends sat transfixed — perhaps in disbelief; it was hard to tell from offstage — while Stevie belted out "I Just Can't Wait to Be King." Occasionally, he was in tune and relatively close to the actual beat. I took a deep breath and whispered "wimoweh" several times to keep my vocal cords limber in readiness for Timon's entrance after Mufasa's tragic death. I still had a little time before that. I could not sit still, however, and the first act of the play had done little to settle my nerves.

Stevie fell off Pride Rock twice. The second time, he cried for a full minute until Boris inched over from his Rock No. 2 spot to settle him down. Brandon's Scar was not bad, but he seemed to be making up the dialogue. Jessica was texting whenever she didn't have a line. The low point came when Mufasa, a.k.a. Henson, bumped into Boris, who in his Rock No. 2 costume doesn't have the best balance owing to his arms being tucked in. Boris tipped over into Zebra No. 1, who fell into Gazelle No. 2, and both of them tumbled into a hippo and three flamingos. Fortunately, complete disaster was averted when Boris sprang to his feet and threw himself against Pride Rock to stop it from falling into the audience.

I was standing in the wings of the stage next to Boris as we watched Stevie's trainwreck of a performance in the second act.

Mr. Hurley came over. He wore a lime-green T-shirt with the caption "Be the Genghis — Experience the Rush."

"Are you trying to wreck the play single-handedly, Snodbuckle?" Mr. Hurley said. "Did you have to push everyone over?"

"I'm sorry, Mr. Hurley. Someone ... knocked into me," Boris said quietly.

Robert and Michael snickered.

"I don't know why I bother," Mr. Hurley muttered. He went back to his chair and opened his red notebook.

"That was a fine bit of footwork to catch Pride Rock," I said to Boris.

"It wouldn't have fallen if I hadn't bashed into Zebra Number One. I made a complete mess of things," Boris said, crestfallen.

The wildebeests left too soon and trampled Simba and Scar together, missing Mufasa altogether. This raised serious questions about how Mufasa would be killed.

"Someone put a stake in my heart and end my suffering," Mr. Hurley said, the back of his hand pressing against his forehead.

Henson began improvising Mufasa's death by pretending to have a heart attack, followed by severe convulsions and a number of violent somersaults and body rolls.

Clearly, it was not going to be a quick death.

"I think a lack of rehearsal time is the real problem," I said to Boris.

Boris nodded slowly. "Not to criticize, but I don't think Mr. Hurley wanted to do this play, and ... maybe he rushed it. How many times did he tell us he was a professional and had more important things to do?"

I did a quick calculation. "Probably five times every rehearsal, and he came to two out of six, about eight times at the audition and then tonight probably another twelve times, so that's ..."

"I didn't really mean for you to figure it out," Boris said.

Boris has tried to teach me not to take things so literally. I obviously have to work on it.

"This isn't fair to the artsy kids," Boris continued. "They look forward to the play every year, and every year it gets worse. The eighth graders didn't even try out! If Mr. Hurley doesn't care, someone else should be the director." He looked around to make sure Mr. Hurley couldn't hear. "I found out Ms. Holmes, the new English teacher, is actually an actor — a real one — a professional; she acted on Broadway in New York and was in movies and on television. I think she was the one Mr. Hurley was talking about when I ..." His voice trailed off.

Neither of us would speak directly about that dark day when he lost his "ouch."

"If I'm president, I'm going to make sure Ms. Holmes directs the play next year," Boris said.

"What do you mean by 'if I'm president'? You will be!" I said.

We gripped forearms. The Roman handshake had survived Operation Rally in the Valley.

Boris gave me a wistful look. "The artsy crowd obviously thinks I'm a joke. Rock Number Two? And I lost my only line, my word. I'll never get their votes. I've already lost the little kids and the Green Goblins to Robert. I'm running out of groups!"

"You still have a good shot with the brainiacs at the Science Fair," I said. "All we need to do is think about the popular kids. Should I come to the War Room tomorrow to brainstorm?"

"No can do. Dad made me paint my room to cover up the marker and it smells too bad right now. But don't worry. The writing shows through the paint."

That was a relief. The campaign could not afford another setback.

Boris tugged on my tail and pointed onstage, pain etched across his face.

Mufasa had finally died. The wildebeests stormed back across the stage and trampled him, which apparently brought him back to life. He jumped up and ran after the wildebeests, threatening to beat them up. Ms. Crimpet had to run across the stage to intervene.

Mr. Hurley was now crying.

Frieda stormed over. She would be wonderful in the role of a fierce warrior princess. She lifted her right foot and pounded the floor in fury. I forced myself not to cry out when her heel crunched my toes.

"I can't believe I agreed to be in this joke of a play. I told you Stevie would mess up. Hurley should have given you the part, Snodbuckle."

"I have to agree with you," I said.

"How can I build my extracurriculars for college and

show that I have lots of interests if everything's going to be as embarrassing as this? All I can add to my resumé from this year is that I won the Science Fair."

"Um ... Science Fair is *next* week," I said softly.

"Yeah. Like there's a doubt how it will turn out," Frieda said confidently. "I've won the last five years, and I should've in first grade, only the judge didn't understand the second law of thermodynamics."

She had a point. Her exhibit that year had been worthy of victory. She'd invented a waterless toilet for use in sub-Saharan Africa. I believe she went on to patent her invention and has since sold it in over thirty countries.

"Are you entering this year?" she asked me.

"I thought I might," I said.

"I didn't think you would since you don't come to the Science Club anymore."

I had suggested to Boris that it would be interesting to test the frictional coefficient of butter by sliding across a buttered classroom floor in our bare feet. It was interesting, but it also led to a two-day suspension for me and Boris. The real tragedy was our lifetime ban from the Science Club.

"Could we have one genuine moment on this stage tonight — just one?" Mr. Hurley said.

"Perhaps we could talk about that later," Ms. Crimpet said quietly. "The audience ... and the cast ... can hear you."

Ms. Crimpet was normally a very calm person. She appeared a bit stressed at the moment.

Jonah tugged on my tail. "I feel sick," he whispered to me. "I don't think I can go on."

This was unwelcome news. Timon without Pumbaa is like a peanut butter sandwich without the peanut butter ... or the bread. My nerves kicked in, which immediately raised the possibility of hyperventilation. "You don't happen to have a paper bag I can breathe into?" I asked Boris.

"I knew you'd fall apart," Michael said gleefully. "Like when you cried in first grade after I broke your stupid pencil."

I really wish he'd let that go.

"He's fine," Boris snapped. "It's just a joke we have."

"Boys are so weird," Frieda said.

I gave Boris a grateful look. Better Frieda think boys are weird than have her glimpse the fear in my soul. I couldn't bear the thought of losing the respect of the only girl I'd ever loved who didn't know that I loved her. That would be almost as painful as listening to Scar butcher his lines.

"Run away. Run away and never come back ... to the place ... in the jungle ... where you go and meet those two guys ... and grow up real fast, like in one song, and then meet Nala and fall in love, and then come back to Pride Rock and fight me and the hyenas ... Oh, yeah, I forgot, you meet the monkey, too."

It was time for Young Simba to exit, but Stevie's stage fright had apparently taken away his ability to move. The play ground to a halt. Mr. Hurley didn't notice. He was writing in his red notebook. Ms. Crimpet was motioning frantically for Stevie to get off stage. The crowd began tittering — and then laughing out loud.

Jonah tugged my tail again. A tear rolled down his cheek. "I can't go on," he whimpered.

Boris put his arm around Jonah's shoulders. "There's nothing to be scared of," he said. "Imagine everyone in the audience is in their underwear."

Ms. Crimpet put on a hippopotamus head and went onstage to rescue Stevie. I collected myself. It was Timon and Pumbaa time.

"I forgot my lines," Jonah said in a panic. "I'm not doing it."

"We're on," I said, with a significant amount of urgency.

"You do it," Jonah said. "I hate that song, anyway."

He threw his headpiece to the floor — a red baseball cap with two long, pointy ears attached to the sides — sat down and crossed his arms.

Stage fright happens, and I was sympathetic to Jonah's plight. It came at a bad time for me, however. I had to be onstage and sing a duet — by myself. My chest was beginning to constrict, the second sign of hyperventilation. I took a few tentative steps forward. All eyes were on me. I looked back. Frieda was watching me intensely. Normally, I would have enjoyed her attention. At present, it added unwanted fuel to the hyperventilation fire. Stevie was hitting himself on the head with his tail. Mr. Hurley ripped a piece of paper from his red notebook. Ms. Crimpet looked on, crestfallen, hippo head in hand.

Boris, my best friend, my mentor, was nowhere to be seen.

I have spent more time alone than I'd like to admit,

in the library or at home after school — when Boris was otherwise occupied, naturally. Yet for all that, I'd never felt more alone than in this moment. As hard as I tried, I couldn't picture the audience members in their undergarments. They remained fully clothed. Instead, I pictured myself in my underwear, with everyone laughing at me.

My throat constricted — hyperventilation sign three.

This was the most humiliating experience of my life.

Suddenly, the melodious chant of "Wimoweh" floated across the stage and the music started. I gasped for breath. Boris wore Jonah's hat, and he had fashioned the rest of the warthog costume out of a garbage bag, tin foil, a backpack and a sweatshirt. It wasn't entirely accurate, but it was beautiful, at least to me.

We locked arms and moved to center stage and began to sing. The audience began to clap, Frieda along with them, her adorable face graced with a smile.

Wimoweh, Wimoweh, Wimoweh, Wimoweh …

CHAPTER NINETEEN

"I don't really need to go," I said to Boris. "It's late already and ... I could use a good night's sleep and ... it's late and ... my science exhibit needs more work ..."

"No chance!" Boris said. "You can't miss the wrap party. You were one of the stars. Everyone'll be there. And the cast always has a wrap party after the show — you told me that yourself. Everyone will be bummed if you're not there."

I had significant doubts about that. "My science experiment is really behind schedule," I offered.

"*You're* behind schedule?" Boris said. "I haven't even started yet." He laughed and, clapping me on the back, led me to the stage where Ms. Crimpet had organized the event.

I approached with caution. In group social situations, I've learned to keep to the background, preferably leaning against a wall. Boris tends not to follow this strategy, especially after a few juices, and at times this has been a problem, like at Christopher Bowles's third-grade birthday party when Boris accepted Robert's challenge to juggle. Boris can juggle — sorta — and he managed to do it — sorta — until the cups fell and shattered. Mrs. Bowles burst into tears. The cups had belonged to her recently deceased great-grandmother.

Robert had told Boris the cups were plastic, but Mrs. Bowles had trouble hearing that because of her weeping. My mom had to come early and get us.

Birthday party invitations dried up after that.

I was overjoyed that no one paid us any attention when we walked onto the stage. A few people were hovering around a table trying to grab pizza slices. Most were off to the right watching a pizza-eating contest between Robert and Michael. Frieda was sitting on the edge of the stage reading a book. Ms. Crimpet came over to us.

"I wanted to thank you again, Boris," she said. "Stepping into Jonah's role like that, without even one rehearsal, really saved the show. You did such a good job."

"Thanks," Boris said. "Adrian needed someone to practice his lines with, so I got to know Pumbaa's part pretty well. It was fun."

"Well, I'm very proud of you," she said. "This show has been ... a challenge, what with no time to rehearse ... and other issues ..." Her voice trailed off and she muttered a few more words. "You'd better hurry and get a slice of pizza," she said. "If you wait too much longer, there won't be any left."

She suddenly brightened. "Speaking of food, that reminds me. To kick off the Kids for a Better Tomorrow Society, I'm organizing a group of students to go to Corktown to participate in the World Youth Hunger Conference — kids who have leadership qualities and an interest in world events. It's a great event where people from all over come to discuss the problem of children going hungry. I wonder if you two would like to go?"

"We'd love it!" Boris said. "Our school needs to do more stuff like that. We gotta get Bendale students helping out in the community. Right now we do practically nothing."

I'd been on the verge of saying yes for myself. Sometimes Boris's enthusiasm makes him speak on my behalf. He was obviously excited, so I pushed it out of my mind.

"Boris is running for president of the student council," I said. "Getting students involved with the community is one of his most important ideas."

"I heard you were running," she said. "I think you'd be a wonderful president." A strange look came over her face. "Robert Pinsent has the same idea about community involvement. He gave me one of his flyers. I was ... pleasantly surprised by it. He has some fantastic ideas. He and some of his friends were handing his flyers out to the audience tonight. Perhaps you should have done something like that."

"Maybe," Boris said.

"Well, you're running out of time," she said. "The election is in three weeks. Anyway, I also invited Robert to the conference. I'm sure you'll have a lot to talk about since you're both so passionate about the subject. The limit per school is ten students. I'm inviting some of the younger kids, too."

The doors to the gym were flung open, and Mr. Hurley raced in and sprinted toward the stage. "Ms. Crimpet, I can't find my red notebook!" he screamed. "It's gone. Everyone be quiet. I need you all to start looking — now. Look everywhere. High and low. Turn this school inside out." His face had lost its color.

He grasped Ms. Crimpet's arm. "Help me. We have to organize a search party." He gestured wildly to a group of kids. "You search stage right — everyone else stage left. Then we'll do a sweep of the gym. Leave no stone unturned. Rip the school apart if you have to."

He threw his arms around Ms. Crimpet and began to sob.

She patted him gently on the back. "I'm sure we'll find it, Franklin. There, there. It'll be okay."

He let out a piercing cry.

The cast went back to eating their pizza.

"I guess we should look around a bit," Boris said to me. "He does sound kinda upset."

"It's like I've lost a loved one — or my heart has been ripped from my chest," Mr. Hurley lamented.

"Maybe we should start looking," Ms. Crimpet said, pulling him offstage — rather forcefully.

"Oh, Genghis! Oh, Flipity-Dipity. Where art thou?" he wailed.

I noticed Robert had been watching Mr. Hurley the entire time. As soon as he and Ms. Crimpet left the stage, Robert let loose the slyest of smiles.

"Hey, I got a joke," Robert said. "Anyone wanna hear it?"

"Sure," Michael said. He attempted to mimic Robert's sly look.

"Why did Rock Number Two cross the road?" Robert said.

A few giggles sounded.

"I do not know," Michael said.

"To knock over the zebra and ruin the play," Robert said.

Michael bent over with laughter. Wong, Henson and Daniels did likewise. Stevie and Jonah grinned away. The rest of the cast looked uncomfortable, and after a few seconds, a gloomy silence prevailed.

Then I heard the famous Snodbuckle laugh, so full of joy, so kindhearted, so real, I had to laugh, too. Had to. No human can resist the B-Ster's good humor.

It can't be done.

And then, as quickly as Robert's joke killed the mood, Boris turned the depressing quiet into roaring laughter. Michael joined in, but uneasily. Robert was totally confused, his smile strained, his eyes wide-open. Stevie and Jonah were laughing so hard they dropped to their knees.

Boris began to sing "The Circle of Life" in his clear, strong baritone, and everyone joined in.

What a perfect way to wrap up a wrap party.

After we finished the song, I wandered to the back of the stage. The kids were talking to one another, and I felt a bit out of place.

"You wanna go?" Boris said, coming over to me.

"I suppose — if you do."

"Okay, let's go." He picked up his backpack.

"What you got there, Bot-Snuckle?"

Robert ripped Boris's backpack out of his hands and tossed it to Michael.

"Real funny, Robert," Boris said. "We gotta go."

Michael threw the bag to Wong, who tossed it to Henson, who punted it back to Daniels.

"You guys making a point by beating up my backpack?" Boris said.

"Yeah. We're proving you're a freaky Buckle Snuckle," Robert said.

"Yeah, a freaky Snuckle Luckle Duckle Buckle," Michael said.

"I know you want me to chase it," Boris said.

"I know you're a loser," Robert said.

Tough to explain what happened next. My brain snapped like a twig, like something went off, a light switch or something, because I charged across the stage at Daniels like the rampaging wildebeests of Act One.

Less enjoyable was tripping over Michael's outstretched foot and crashing to the stage floor on my knees and rolling on my back in excruciating pain while everyone laughed at me.

"Why'd you do that?" Boris yelled. He knelt beside me. "You really hurt him. Are you always such a jerk?"

"You're the professional jerk around here," Michael said.

"I wonder what he's got in his backpack that's so important," Robert said.

Daniels threw it to him. Robert unzipped it slowly.

And he pulled out Mr. Hurley's red notebook.

"I am so disappointed in you, Boris. I am very, very, very disappointed," Robert said.

"I didn't put it there," Boris said angrily. "Are you okay?" he asked me.

"I think so," I said.

I could see Frieda looking at me.

And I could feel her disdain — a pathetic boy lying on the stage in front of everyone.

Boris helped me up.

"Mr. Hurley," Robert yelled. "Mr. Hurley. I found it."

Mr. Hurley ran to him. "You're a hero!" He covered the red notebook in kisses. "Where'd you find it?" he asked Robert.

"I don't really want to tell you. I don't want to get the kid who took it in trouble," Robert said.

I had no idea Robert followed the Code.

"You will tell me and you will tell me right now. I must get to the bottom of this horrendous crime," Mr. Hurley said.

"He found it in my backpack," Boris said.

Mr. Hurley staggered backward. "You're a monster," he said.

"We should just forget about it," Robert said. "I think Boris was a bit mad at you because you took away his one word, his 'ouch.' He's sorry about it, right, Boris? You're sorry for taking Mr. Hurley's red notebook, aren't you? The important thing is I found it."

"I will not stand for this criminal behavior," Mr. Hurley began.

"I think Robert is right," Ms. Crimpet interrupted.

I'd never heard her speak with such force.

"The notebook has been found, and it doesn't matter how," Ms. Crimpet said. "Parents are waiting to pick up their kids. Okay, everyone. Great show. We're proud of all of you. Let's collect our things and get going. Your parents are in the Teachers' Lounge." Ms. Crimpet gave Mr. Hurley a serious stare. He took a step back from her and cleared his voice.

"I can understand the pain of losing a line — or a word. Who more than me understands the pressure of performing on a stage. I forgive you, Boris," Mr. Hurley said. "I won't forget the bravery of this young boy here, though." He put a hand on Robert's shoulder. "This young boy will be celebrated. We will have an assembly, and we will honor this fine person with the … the … the Artistic Bravery Award." Mr. Hurley clutched his red notebook to his chest. "I must tell your parents what you've done. Are they waiting for you?"

"They should be in the Teachers' Lounge," Robert said.

They left the stage together. Ms. Crimpet let out a sigh and began to clean up.

Michael threw the backpack at Boris's feet, and he along with Wong, Henson and Daniels followed Mr. Hurley and Robert.

"Are you, um, okay to walk?" Boris asked me.

I'd totally forgotten about my knees. "Of course. It — it wasn't that bad."

I said it loudly, in the hope that Frieda would be impressed by my ability to handle pain. She didn't seem overly interested. Instead, she watched Mr. Hurley and Robert.

Robert Pinsent — I cursed his very name. Every time I turned around, it seemed Robert was being crowned a king by someone. The primary kids and the Green Goblins had already been lost, and now Boris had been discredited in front of the artsy crowd, with Mr. Hurley arranging an assembly for Robert's artistic achievements.

Boris's Pumbaa was long forgotten.

Now the artsy crowd would remember Boris as the ouch-less Rock No. 2 — and a notebook stealer.

And Frieda would remember me as the bumbling buffoon who fell down chasing a backpack.

PART V

Operation Triple-R

CHAPTER TWENTY

The Science Fair was scheduled to start promptly at nine o'clock. I'd spoken to Boris last night at around seven, and he'd told me he'd be working through the night to get his exhibit ready on time. I offered to help, but Boris said that would be cheating. He also wanted his exhibit to be a surprise for me.

Who doesn't like a good surprise?

My first surprise didn't involve Boris, however. I might even call it an unpleasant surprise, and it came in the form of Robert Pinsent pushing a cart with a midsized cardboard box on it, with Michael Beverley traipsing after him. Their entrance created quite the buzz. The Science Fair doesn't usually attract Bendale's A-listers.

"So where do you want us to set up, Ms. C.?" Robert asked.

Ms. Crimpet looked at her clipboard. "I'm sorry, Robert. I don't have your name as an exhibitor. When did you sign up?"

"Gosh, Ms. Crimpet. I signed up ages ago. You mean I can't be in the Science Fair? I've always wanted to participate, but I was always too scared. I love science, and I thought it would be cool to show my science work and maybe even join the Science Club. Michael, how awesome would it be to hang with my science bros and do science stuff?"

"About the most awesome thing ever," Michael said.

A few girls giggled. Several members of the Science Club looked terribly pleased at the announcement that Robert and Michael wished to join. Frieda balled her fists. She had her warrior eyes going full blast.

"Well ... You're certainly enthusiastic, which is nice," Ms. Crimpet said. "All the places are taken, but if you want to set up in the back you can —"

"This spot is fine," Robert said.

"Hi, Frieda," Robert said breezily.

Frieda muttered something under her breath.

Robert ran a hand through his hair and grinned ever so devilishly.

"Thanks a lot. You're the best, Ms. C.," Robert said.

"Could we get started," the Principal said to Ms. Crimpet. "We don't want to keep Mr. Sheckle waiting."

Mr. Sheckle was a fairly disheveled man, with a baggy beige suit, no tie, brown shoes and patches of stringy hair that formed the faintest of head coverings. He held up a large coffee and grunted, which I assumed meant that he agreed the Science Fair should start.

Ms. Crimpet cleared her throat. "It's still only eight forty-five. We have fifteen minutes, and a registered student hasn't arrived."

"Who?"

"Boris — Boris Snodbuckle."

The Principal gasped, choked, swallowed hard several times, blinked repeatedly and finished with several hand swoops across his brow. "We can't wait," he said. "Impossible. Time is too valuable — and ... the spots are all taken — and ... Boris is registered?"

The gym doors flew open. Boris entered wearing a T-shirt and a pair of swim shorts, a shower cap and goggles, pulling a small blue recycling bin behind him. An ill-mannered fool (I suspect Stevie) whispered loudly, "Buckle Head is gonna burn the school down." Boris rose above it.

"Sorry I'm late. I had a problem with a pump, and then I had to fill up my bins. Where should I set up?" Boris asked Ms. Crimpet. A bit of water splashed out of the bin. Boris wiped it up with his shirt.

"I suppose you'll have to set up in the back against the far wall," Ms. Crimpet said. "Sorry, Boris. Someone took your place." She gave Robert and Michael a stern look.

"No worries," Boris said. "I brought some extra rope in case." He gave her a carefree smile and a quick double eyebrow flick to me, and then pulled his bin to the far wall.

"I suppose we can get going," Ms. Crimpet said to the Principal.

"Boys and girls, may I have your complete and undivided attention," the Principal began. "The Science Fair will now start." Ms. Crimpet pulled on his sleeve and pointed to the banner hanging on the wall. The Principal cleared his throat. "Excuse me, the Bendale Triple-R Science-Palooza will now start."

Ms. Crimpet pointed to the gong on the table. The Principal gave it a most impressive strike.

Ms. Crimpet stepped forward. "Welcome, students, to the Bendale Triple-R Science-Palooza," she announced. "I wish you the best of luck. You will each have five minutes to present your exhibit to the judges and to answer questions. After we've seen everyone, we'll take another few minutes to vote and then we'll announce the winners. Remember, this is for fun, and it doesn't really matter who gets a ribbon. You're all winners as far as we're concerned. Now let me introduce our generous sponsor, Mr. Herman Sheckle of ..." She looked at a piece of paper. "Mr. Herman Sheckle of Sheckle, Minx and Associates — Real Estate and Insurance Adjusters, at 147 Heathcote Avenue. I believe a round of applause is in order."

Some tentative clapping followed, and the Science Fair was under way. I steeled my nerves for the fierce competition ahead. I looked over at Frieda's exhibit. This year she'd ventured into the field of electromagnetism, or what most think of as really strong magnets, and she was investigating its potential in the transportation and mining industries. It was another impressive display of her genius.

Boris left the gym and then returned with another small recycling bin. The judges began with Stevie and Jonah. Their exhibit was so pathetic I felt sorry for them. They had suspended a rock over a soda pop can with a string. Stevie cut the string, and the rock fell and crushed the can. They called it the Can Crusher. I couldn't watch and instead slipped over to see how Boris was making out. He'd just returned a third time with Gordie, who was loaded down with extension cords, hoses, duct tape, rope, metallic clips and a machine that looked like an air compressor, a device that pumps out air under pressure.

"I was getting worried. Why were you so late?" I asked.

Boris's face was drawn and tired. He'd obviously been hard at it last night getting his exhibit ready. "I couldn't get the clips to hold. Finally, I had to borrow my dad's power drill, and then he woke up and took it away, so I had to sneak into his bedroom to get it back and use all the extension cords in the house to do the work in the backyard so he wouldn't hear. Then Chaz started barking, and I had to go back and make him a steak, which he really liked, by the way. It's a miracle I even finished."

It was nice to hear that he and Chaz were becoming friendlier. But my curiosity was positively raging about his exhibit.

"You certainly have a lot of equipment," I said.

"Yup," he answered.

"Looks like an air compressor. Pumping something up with air?"

"Yup."

"Does it have to do with those bins?"

"Yup." He began to grin. He clipped the bins shut. "I'm not gonna tell you, Adrian. It's a surprise."

The judges were edging closer to my exhibit.

"Good luck, Boris!" I said. I held out my arm.

"Good luck to you, too, Adrian," he said, looking me square in the eye.

We grasped arms, and I hurried back to my exhibit. The judges were just finishing up with Frieda.

"This is absolutely wonderful," Ms. Crimpet said to Frieda several times.

"Amazing. Just amazing," the Principal said.

They came to my exhibit.

"This is Adrian," Ms. Crimpet said, "and his solar-powered train. And look, he's also built an entire miniature city to go with it."

"Solar! The future's in nuclear power," the Principal said.

"Nothing wrong with good honest coal either," Mr. Sheckle said. "My dad used coal to heat his house until they forced him to switch to a gas furnace. Good enough for him; good enough for me. Solar? That's a pipe dream. Solar power costs too much. The sun is too far away."

Their comments did not augur well for my entry. "There have been tremendous advances in solar panel technology," I offered. "As you can see from this chart, the energy output per panel ..."

"Okay, sure. I can see," Mr. Sheckle said, as he looked at his phone.

Out of the corner of my eye, I saw Boris attach a hose from the air compressor to a hole in the top of the bins.

"Any questions?" Ms. Crimpet said.

Mr. Sheckle grimaced. "How much longer?" he asked.

"We have two more exhibitors," Ms. Crimpet said. "Principal?"

"Well done, Adrian, but you should research nuclear energy," the Principal said.

"Nuclear energy poses serious environmental risks," I said, "as demonstrated by several accidents over the past four decades, including ..."

The need to continue the debate faded with each step the Principal and Mr. Sheckle took toward Robert and Michael's exhibit.

"Good work, Adrian. It's a well-researched and well-implemented piece of science," Ms. Crimpet said to me. She seemed unhappy about something. "Coal," she muttered disgustedly as she left.

The evidence was undeniable: two of the three judges were unimpressed with my exhibit. Even if Ms. Crimpet threw her support behind me, I had no chance. Frieda was a formidable opponent, but I had thought this was my best entry yet. The blue ribbon would not be mine — a bitter pill after all my work.

CHAPTER TWENTY-ONE

Robert and Michael lifted the cardboard box to reveal a square unit covered in brown wrapping paper.

"It's just a prototype," Robert said. "It's not totally done. I have a few more bugs to work out. But anyway, this is the Super-Duper Mega-Whooper Trash Compactor. It takes garbage and crushes it up into tiny bits. We could reduce the size of the garbage we toss in a landfill by seven times — I mean it."

"Amazing," the Principal said. "Isn't that amazing, Mr. Sheckle?"

Mr. Sheckle was occupied with his phone and didn't answer.

"I have some typical household garbage in this bag," Robert said, holding it up for the judges to see. "I will now put the garbage in the Super-Duper Mega-Whooper Trash Compactor and …" He and Michael stood in front of their exhibit, so I couldn't quite see what they were doing, although from the sound of it they were dumping the garbage into their device.

With dramatic flourish, Robert held up his index finger and proclaimed, "For science and the environment." Then he bent over and poked the top of the device.

A loud grinding noise followed. Robert took the time to show off his pearly white teeth and flip his wavy hair a few times with the tips of his fingers.

"That should do it," he said.

Again, he and Michael stood in front to obscure our view. Robert whirled around holding a tiny cube of what looked like very compressed garbage.

"Could you tell me how this is powered?" Ms. Crimpet said. She looked confused.

"It's solar powered," Robert said. "That was the hardest part to figure out."

"Amazing," the Principal said. "Isn't it amazing, Mr. Sheckle?"

Mr. Sheckle's response was muffled by the donut in his mouth.

I admit I was floored. Robert's exhibit was impressive — a solar-powered trash compactor, fully functioning. Such devices existed, but they were very expensive and made in real factories. To create one from scratch would require machine parts, electronics, software and a thorough understanding of the principles of physics and photovoltaics, the latter being the method of converting solar power into electricity.

"I'd like to take a closer look at your work and research, if I could," Ms. Crimpet said.

Robert and Michael stepped in front of their exhibit.

"I've taken up a lot of your time already," Robert said. "Maybe you should see the last exhibit."

"Yes, but I would like to —"

"He's right," the Principal said. "Come along, Ms. Crimpet. Mr. Sheckle was good enough to sponsor this event. We shouldn't impose on him too much."

Mr. Sheckle stuffed the rest of his donut into his mouth and nodded.

"I just need one moment," Ms. Crimpet said.

"Judges, please, if you will," Boris sang out. "Come forward. No need to be afraid. No cause for alarm." He waved at the judges from the back wall.

Ms. Crimpet paused and then followed the Principal and Mr. Sheckle to Boris. I joined them.

"I have tackled the problem of wasting water," Boris declared, and he pointed to the Principal. "Any idea how much water we waste every time we take a shower? Take a guess."

The Principal stared at him.

Boris swung to his right. "How about you, kind sir?" he said to Mr. Sheckle. "Would you care to take a guess at the amount of wasted H_2O?"

Mr. Herman Sheckle's right eye began to twitch. "Nah, kid. No idea."

"You wouldn't believe me if I told you. But I'll tell you anyway."

Boris is a natural showman. Robert may have put together a first-class exhibit, but I knew he was about to learn a thing or two about performing for an audience.

I'd seen it firsthand in first grade. Boris and I had not met yet, at least not formally — had hardly exchanged a word, in fact. On that day, Boris brought a helium balloon from home. The teacher had stepped out to speak to the Principal, and Boris called the entire class to gather around. We were mesmerized as he tied the balloon to his waist, climbed onto his desk and announced his desire to see if he could float. Who hasn't wanted to test that out?

Of course, we soon discovered that one balloon

couldn't hold his weight. He landed heavily. And unfortunately he broke his leg. The silver lining was that the teacher asked me to sit with Boris until the ambulance came to take him to the hospital.

We've been best friends ever since.

CHAPTER TWENTY-TWO

It didn't surprise me that my fellow exhibitors quickly formed a semicircle around me and the judges. I took a closer look: two recycling bins were leaning forward, held in place by several pieces of wood and ropes attached to a basketball net.

"In North America, the average shower uses seventeen gallons of water, depending on the pressure," Boris said. He pointed to a chart on a piece of Bristol board. It was unfortunate that his black marker had begun to run out of ink and it was hard to see the numbers.

"How would you know? You've never taken a shower," Robert said.

Stevie, Jonah and Michael enjoyed that joke thoroughly.

"Brushing your teeth can use up to half a gallon, and that's if you don't leave the water running," Boris said.

Interesting facts, but where was Boris going with this?

"Is that not a staggering waste of water — and just plain dumb?" Boris asked the crowd.

"About as dumb as you," Robert said.

Boris responded with an understanding smile. "What would you say if I told you I can shower up to twenty kids and three adults with less than one hundred gallons of water, and also have them all brush their teeth? And what would you say if I showed you how?" He switched the compressor on.

That shut Robert up.

"That would be something," Ms. Crimpet said.

The Principal's right eye twitched nervously.

Boris took a container from Gordie and twisted off the lid. "Pass these toothbrushes around and get a good helping of toothpaste. Take a few steps forward. It's showtime in three minutes," Boris exclaimed.

If excitement could be measured in temperature, it would have been 120 degrees Fahrenheit. As each second ticked by, the buzz from the crowd grew louder and louder. I did some rough calculations. Twenty kids taking a shower would use about 250 to 300 gallons of water. Three adults would add about 50 more. If Boris could truly shower twenty kids and three adults with only 100 gallons of water, he would cut consumption by a whopping 70 percent, give or take. That would be an astonishing accomplishment.

"It is time!" Boris said, throwing his arms wide apart. "Please begin to brush your teeth, and when I give the command, open your mouths." He waited another thirty seconds and then took the rope attached to the lids firmly in his hands.

"Open your mouths!" he yelled.

We did. He yanked the rope, and the clips holding the bin lids flew off. The lids sprang open and water flew out. I suddenly got it. Such simplicity. The air compressor created a pressurized system in the bins.

When the lids opened, the water had only one place to go — out. The bins had been angled so the water would spray forward. We were covered in water, and we were showered, with enough water in our mouths to rinse the toothpaste away.

We were also soaking wet, including the Principal, Ms. Crimpet and Mr. Sheckle. Boris alone remained dry.

Boris looked positively thrilled. "Instant group shower," he said. "One hundred gallons of water and you're all clean. You could soap up and then with maybe one more bin you could rinse."

He held his hand out for Ms. Crimpet to shake. She squeezed water from her hair.

"I got the idea after I saw my neighbor's dog, Chaz, swimming in their hot tub," Boris said. "When he was finished, he shook his body real fast and hard, and water went flying in all directions. I got to thinking about how we could use water like that, and then I thought of my shower. The hard part was figuring out a way to get the water to cover people since I don't have a dog's body to shake, although I did think of maybe getting a pack of dogs and —"

"Snodbuckle — to my office!" the Principal thundered.

Boris flashed a look of concern. "I know you got a bit wet, but I wanted to try and figure out something that would really help people."

"You want to help? Go to a different school," Robert said. He tossed his toothbrush at Boris.

Mr. Sheckle pulled his phone from his pocket. "He

got this wet," he growled to the Principal. "You're gonna buy me a new one — and you're paying to get this suit dry-cleaned. It's brand-new."

I wondered what kind of store sold brand-new suits that looked so old and tattered, and I also wondered what damage this might do to Boris's campaign. My fellow exhibitors seemed to be taking their cue from Robert.

"You're the all-time leading doofus, Buckle Behind," Robert said. "Your exhibit takes stupid to outer space."

"Yeah. It's stupid," Michael said.

"Can you please begin to clean up your exhibits," Ms. Crimpet said quietly. "We'll announce the winners later … when we've had a chance to dry off."

I figured Boris needed some alone time. I went back to my exhibit. I looked over and noticed Frieda brooding, water dripping from her clothes, and to her right, Robert's Super-Duper Mega-Whooper Trash Compactor. Something about it bothered me. I just couldn't understand how he'd done it. Ms. Crimpet had left, presumably to towel off. The Principal was talking to Robert and Michael. Mr. Sheckle seemed to have disappeared.

My curiosity could not be contained. I needed to know.

I walked toward Robert's exhibit.

A bony hand gripped my shoulder.

I had never experienced the joy of Frieda's touch before — and always imagined it would be far less painful.

"Snodbuckle came up with that without you?" Frieda asked me.

"Yes."

"Hmm. It's a rather crude delivery system, and it wastes water because of the uncontrolled trajectory of liquid shooting out from a recycling bin, but I'm impressed he's thinking about saving water. It's an important issue," she said.

Normally, I relish the chance to discuss Boris's great ideas, and quality time with Frieda is hard to come by. Unfortunately, I had business to attend to.

"It is, but ... um ... excuse me, Frieda, I just need to ... do something."

Frieda shrugged and began packing up her exhibit. I made my way over to Robert's exhibit.

I tapped the sides — an echo. I tapped louder — again an echo. That meant two things: the inside was hollow and the box was made of a very hard and smooth material, possibly a metallic substance. I picked at the brown paper and ripped the corner ever so slightly — and saw something shiny and metal. I pulled more paper away.

Stainless steel! I opened the top and gasped.

The box was empty, except for a laptop covered by some garbage.

Of course! They'd faked the entire thing. Robert was a fraud! They'd used a small garbage can and covered it in paper. Then they threw garbage into the can and pulled out garbage that had already been pressed into a cube. The laptop provided the sound effects.

Solar powered — my foot!

Solar-powered fakery more like it!

Outraged, I marched over to Boris.

"You won't believe it!" I said to Boris.

He was loading some ropes onto Gordie.

"Hey, Adrian. Looks like I messed up again."

"Messed up? I loved it. Sure, we got a bit wet, but so what? That's what science is about. Experimenting, failing and starting over again. It gets messy."

"But the brainiacs don't think so."

"They do. They're just a little wet right now," I said. "Listen." I put my mouth close to his ear. "Robert's exhibit is a fake. I saw it. It doesn't work."

He stood tall. "You sure about that?"

"Saw it myself. It's an empty metal box covered in paper."

His eyes took on a faraway look, his lips pursed in deep concentration mode. "We can't say anything," he said finally.

"But why?" I gasped.

"Rule Five," he said, not without a hint of melancholy. "I can't tattle to get Robert into trouble. I can only tattle to get someone out of trouble. No one's in trouble here. So it's up to the judges to find out."

I struggled to find a counterargument — and then gave in.

Once again, Robert's treachery would go unpunished.

The Code, so near and dear to my heart, was becoming a real pain!

"Students, can I have your attention," Ms. Crimpet announced. "I'd like to announce the winners. Mr. Sheckle had to go." She cleared her throat. "The winner is Robert Pinsent for his Super-Duper Mega … Whooper Trash Compactor."

A hearty cheer rose up. Robert shook hands with the Principal and went to collect the first-place blue ribbon. Frieda spun on her heels and left the gym. Ms. Crimpet watched her go for a moment before continuing. "Frieda is second. I'll give her the award later. Stevie and Jonah are third for their can crusher."

I'd lost out to a fake exhibit and a rock held by a string.

Boris had soaked the elite members of the brainiacs and was possibly headed for another suspension.

I could hardly wait for this election to be over.

PART VI

Operation Feed
the World

CHAPTER TWENTY-THREE

I knocked gently. Boris opened the War Room's window. His face was flushed with excitement. From the writing on the wall, I could see he'd been busy over the past two days during his Science Fair suspension. He'd texted me to come over and see his newest idea to win the election. I was excited to hear the plan.

"I was a bit down after the Science Fair. I know I'm not a brainiac, but I wanted to show them that I like how you guys use your brains to make awesome things that help the world. I guess they weren't too happy about getting wet. I thought I'd blown it, and Robert would be president and there was nothing I could do to stop him. Then it hit me — *HOLISTICS!*"

Intrigued — yes.

Understanding — no.

"I'm not really familiar with that word," I said tentatively.

"Remember when you gave a presentation at school last year?" he said, as I climbed through the window. "You told us how we have lots of food to feed everyone five times over. The problem is *holistics.*"

"I believe I said *logistics* — the coordination of a series of complicated tasks in the best way possible, in this case sending food from one country that has extra food to another country with a shortage. And I think I made that presentation in third grade," I said.

He paused. "So … what's that word again?"

"Logistics."

"Exactly. Ms. Crimpet gave me the idea when she told us about that World Youth Hunger Conference. I got to thinking about the election and that things weren't going all that well, what with the little kids, the Green Goblins, the artsy kids and the brainiacs all probably voting for Robert. But that still leaves the popular kids, and I thought that maybe all they need is a better way to spend their time, like working together to make Bendale a better school or helping the community, and then they'd be too busy to bother with bullying or wedgies."

"It would be nice to end the Wedgie War," I mused. "And the plan is?"

"The plan is really yours and Ms. Crimpet's. I'm gonna feed a bunch of hungry kids at the conference, and once the popular kids find out about it, maybe they'll change their minds about me. Maybe some of the little kids, the Green Goblins, the artsy kids and the brainiacs will, too. This could win it for me."

"Maybe."

"So I figured out a way to do it — with logistics. I've spoken to Sandy, and she's gonna do another interview. I'll be in the papers and on TV. I'll be popular, but for the right reason — because I fed hungry kids."

"So how are you going to do it?"

"I worked it all out when I was eating at the Burger Pit."

"Your parents took you to the Burger Pit even though you're on suspension?" I said in amazement.

Boris gave me an odd look. "No. I went with Gordie. Anyway, I looked around at all the trays. Most people didn't finish their food, didn't even touch some of it. We obviously can't collect food that's been served, but I bet restaurants and supermarkets have tons of food that they can't use. We'll collect it and get it to people who are hungry. It'll be like a food bank for the world, feed kids from here to ... far away. Are you with me?"

I saluted.

"Write this out on the wall," Boris said.

1. Set up a website and blog
2. Tweet every twenty minutes to our followers
3. Go to the Burger Pit
4. Serve breakfast to hungry Bendale students — the test run
5. Do interview with Sandy — bring Tic Tacs for Ernie
6. Go to the Munch Mart to get more food
7. Deliver food to the World Youth Hunger Conference
8. Win popular kids over
9. Write speech
10. Win the election

I took a closer look at the list of items and told Boris I could help with number 1.

"Thanks, Adrian. That's what I like about you," Boris said. "You always volunteer to do the hard stuff."

I didn't quite understand why setting up an interactive

website and blog was hard stuff — a little programming, a few paragraphs and pictures each day to keep the content fresh and that was it. Nice of Boris to thank me, though. I tapped my watch.

"You're right," Boris said. "We gotta get to school quick. We're gonna have a busy morning."

I followed Boris out the window. We climbed down the tree and made our way to school. We'd only just locked our bikes when the bell rang.

Boris put a hand on my shoulder. "Would you mind if we missed the national anthem and the announcements again?"

"What about your promise to Mrs. Brundleford? She was very emphatic about being on time," I said.

"I know, and it's killing me. I think we have a Rule Four situation — try your best not to lie. I'll apologize. But right now we need to advertise tomorrow's hunger breakfast. I really think we need to test things out before we try something bigger. A breakfast at school should be easy. We'll start with the primary classes and work our way up. If we see the Principal, let's go with Escape Plan 2A."

Plan 2A called for a sprint to the basement, where we'd take a secret passage, which we'd made by unbolting a wire fence. Then we would go through the boiler room to the elevator, where we'd ride up to the second floor.

After some discussion, we decided to enter at the northeast stairwell where morning traffic is generally the lightest. That's when a terrible piece of bad luck hit. The Principal was standing guard at that very spot. We were caught red-handed.

I was terrified. All I could manage was to stutter, "We b-b-bikes l-l-late."

"Boris Snodbuckle, explain yourself," he said.

"Sorry. Don't have time. We have a million things to do," Boris said.

The Principal ran a hand across his brow, sighed deeply twice and, with an index finger extended at Boris, said slowly, "We met one month ago with your parents, and twice last year, and I spoke to your father on the phone and we exchanged half a dozen emails — and you promised to be on time." He concluded with a final jab of his finger in the air.

The Principal and Boris continued to talk about a variety of subjects until suddenly the Principal threw his hands in the air and gave us a detention. Boris thought it unfair. I suggested the Principal had made some good points, and Boris, being good-natured, came around and agreed that we deserved some form of punishment. We promised to go to class. The Principal went back to his office.

Boris made a right at the bottom of the stairs.

"Our class is the other way," I told him.

"We gotta tell everyone about the breakfast."

"But the Principal ...?"

"I didn't lie. We'll go to class, just not right away. What's the point of having a breakfast for hungry kids if the hungry kids don't know about it?"

That was true. "Are there hungry kids at Bendale?" I asked.

"We'll find out tomorrow at breakfast."

He had me there. "But Mrs. Brundleford ...?"

"Do you think she wants hungry kids at school?"

"I can't imagine she does."

"Then what choice do we have? Besides, the Principal's confused. He already gave me detention this week for the Science Fair." Boris pushed open the door to a third-grade class. "Howdy, third graders," he said. "Say goodbye to hunger at Bendale."

A group of youngsters began chanting "Buckle Butt," until a certain Lynda Skittle silenced them with a piercing glance.

"Who's hungry?" Boris asked.

Every student put up a hand.

I had no idea hunger was such a big problem at Bendale.

CHAPTER TWENTY-FOUR

I rolled up the driveway and leaned my bike against the garage door. The Snodbuckle home showed no signs of life. Granted, Boris and his parents are not early risers — and it was six in the morning. Boris had insisted I come early to make sure we had enough time to transport the food to school for the hunger breakfast. We'd enjoyed tremendous success last night. The Burger Pit's owner was delighted to help "his best little customers." Two other restaurants Boris frequented gave us food as well. We were given so much food we had to make two trips. Gordie did most of the heavy lifting, fortunately. It had been fairly late when we finally loaded the last of it into Boris's garage.

Dampness in the early-morning air contributed to the cool temperature, and I took myself to task for not wearing a sweatshirt. Shivering in Boris's backyard, I hunted around for pebbles to bounce off the War Room window to signal my arrival. Five minutes later, my arm hurt slightly. But the exercise had warmed me up. I began to doubt that Boris was awake. I saw no other option. Up the tree I went, suffering my usual pangs of terror as I inched across the limb to the window.

Boris was fast asleep. I knocked gently.

I debated whether to risk a louder knock, but then decided Boris had been under a great deal of stress lately and needed his rest. I sat on the window frame, my feet pushing against a tree limb, took out my tablet and began to draft today's entry for our blog. I was just about done when the window opened. I got a bit of a fright, and if not for Boris's lightning reflexes, I might have suffered a nasty fall.

"We need to get going," Boris said, pushing his way out. "You should've woken me up."

"Sorry," I said. "I was working on the blog, and you know me when I get writing."

Together we went to the garage and as quietly as possible opened the door.

Boris remained stoic as he surveyed the mayhem and destruction. I marveled at his self-control. Animals of some sort had ransacked the food, and judging by the shape of the paw prints in an apple pie, I suspected raccoons.

"I wonder how they got in," I said.

"Doesn't matter," Boris said.

All of it was ruined, which Boris accepted after a brief discussion over whether food partly eaten by wild animals was fit for human consumption. We had a serious problem. We'd gone to every class in school yesterday and invited any hungry students to come to breakfast in the cafeteria. Now we had nothing to offer.

"Should we cancel?" I said.

Boris's left eye squinted. "Why would we do that?"

I pointed at the mess.

Boris waved his hand in the air. "We know we can get the food. It doesn't matter if the kids don't eat the same food we collected last night. Obviously, we'll store it in a more secure place next time. No big deal. We've got tons of food in the house. We'll use that."

"Do you think your parents have enough food for everyone, and would they want you to take it?"

"You know my parents. Don't you think they'd want us to feed hungry kids?" He tipped Gordie's handle toward me. "Take the Gord-Monster to the back. I'll leave the screen door open. Use Plan Sofa."

Plan Sofa called for me to crawl under the side table, around a cabinet and behind the sofa. We use it when we want to get close to the kitchen without being detected. I went to the back, slipped in and quickly got into position. From there I could see Boris and his dad facing each other.

"Mom told me to tell you there's a huge mess in the garage," Boris said. "It's gross. She's real mad, too," Boris said.

His father held his arms out. "What happened? Why would there be …?" He stopped, and the air seemed to seep slowly out of his body, like a tire with a nail in it. "One morning in my life, I'd like to have my coffee in peace, just once," he muttered as he left.

Boris waved me over. He pulled two duffel bags from a closet and tossed one to me. "Clean out the fridge. I'll go for the cans and bread." He raced to the pantry.

The fridge was full and well organized. Drinks, yogurt and various containers occupied the top shelf; eggs, butter and toppings were on the sides; and various fruits and vegetables filled the drawers. Leftovers in plastic containers were piled somewhat haphazardly. Time was pressing, so I started low and worked my way up. I was surprised by how heavy the bag became. I could not fit everything in, but apart from a few items the fridge was mostly bare.

Boris dragged his bag over to me. It was also full. "Put your bag on Gordie," he whispered. He handed me a can opener. "Hurry."

I had some problems dragging my bag to the back, but I managed. I turned to see Boris pulling madly on his. I ran over and between the two of us we were able to put it on Gordie.

"BORIS!" his dad thundered.

"Let's go," Boris said to me.

Together we hauled Gordie around to the front, hitched him to Boris's bike and set off for school.

"I wonder what your dad wanted to talk to you about," I said.

"Probably wants my advice on something," Boris said.

It's possible, I thought.

Unlikely, but possible.

CHAPTER TWENTY-FIVE

We pedaled hard and arrived at the school in short order. It took some doing to get our trusty Gordie from the parking lot to the doors, but with Boris pulling and me pushing we got it done.

"Hold on," Boris said. He let go of the handle and walked to the bulletin board. After a brief moment his chin drifted to his chest.

This aroused my curiosity, and I went over. A list had been posted with the heading "Students Chosen to Attend the World Youth Hunger Conference." Ms. Crimpet had selected Robert Pinsent, along with students from most grades, including the one and only Lynda Skittle. There were eight students listed — but not Boris or me. The light had faded from Boris's eyes. I felt his pain.

"We can still use logistics to feed hungry kids. We don't have to be invited to a conference to do that, do we?" I said.

Boris pulled his shoulders back and flashed a thumbs-up. "You're right. The point wasn't to get a day off school to go to a conference, and I realize now that I don't have to be president of the student council to make Bendale a better place. Didn't we help the little kids get the swings?"

"Certainly," I said.

"And didn't we help save the Valley, even a little?"

"I'd say more than a little, Octavius."

"And we helped out in the school play."

"Undoubtedly."

"Maybe the Science Fair got a little wet, and they didn't appreciate your solar-powered train, but we were there, right?"

"Absolutely."

"And we won't let this stop us from feeding hungry kids. No chance. I was being selfish. Sorry about that, Adrian."

I was confused to hear the words *selfish* and *Boris* in the same sentence, and so I wasn't able to respond before he grabbed hold of Gordie and pulled him to the cafeteria. Experience has taught me to let the B-Ster have time to himself in extremely emotional moments, so I let him be.

My heart skipped a beat when we entered the lunchroom. The place was packed. Hunger is indeed a very widespread problem at Bendale.

"This better be good, Snodbuckle-Up," Robert sneered.

"I skipped breakfast for this," Michael chirped. "If it sucks, you're dead."

"You check out the list for the conference yet, Brass Buckle?" Robert said.

Boris paid no heed. I adopted Boris's steely-eyed gaze.

"Welcome to Operation Feed the World. This is a test run for my plan to end hunger for kids. Give me a second and you can dig in," Boris said.

He unzipped the two duffel bags and handed me the can opener. "Start opening stuff and I'll set up the buffet," he said to me.

I pulled out a can.

"Is that corn?" Jessica said to Cinny.

I placed two cereal boxes on the table. These are common breakfast items, so they garnered a murmur of approval. I took out two milk cartons next. "Do we have bowls and cutlery?" I whispered to Boris.

"I had to freestyle a bit," Boris said. He handed me a stack of wineglasses, four large mixing bowls and a pile of soupspoons. I poured a carton of milk into a mixing bowl, while Boris laid out a bag of smoked turkey, a jar of pickles and a pack of raisins.

The crowd began to buzz, not in a good way, and the buzzing grew louder and louder. It sounded like they were unhappy. I agree that red kidney beans are rarely eaten at breakfast — but we were trying our best. We were irresponsible for bringing peanut butter — but Juliet Demers went too far when she accused Boris of trying to kill her.

She went screaming out of the cafeteria.

"Come and eat," Boris yelled.

No one moved.

"Did you losers get all this food from your house?" Robert said.

I cursed his powers of deduction under my breath. Boris laughed and popped a kidney bean in his mouth — and then spit it out.

Jonah took a pickle, some raisins and a roasted chicken leg. Stevie helped himself to a handful of

Frosted Flakes. That broke the ice, and the kids descended on the food. Robert and Michael began to fight over a can of root beer. Two other students began a tug-of-war over a slice of cold pizza. I stepped back in fear. The room was beginning to look a lot like Boris's garage, minus the raccoon paw prints.

"We might have to make this a regular thing," Boris said. "These guys are starving. Now we have to prove we can send food anywhere we want."

"How are we going to do that?" I said.

"Hold on, Adrian," Boris said. "Sandy is here."

Sandy and Ernie walked in.

"Boris, you certainly are a busy young man," Sandy said.

"Can't worry about that when there are hungry kids to feed," Boris said.

"Can we do the interview in front of the table?" Sandy said. "And can you get the kids to stop throwing food?"

Stevie was rubbing mustard into Jonah's hair.

"I could try," Boris said, "but you know what hungry kids are like."

The Principal and Mrs. Brundleford came rushing in with Juliet.

"Stop this insanity immediately," the Principal roared.

At that moment, Jonah launched a handful of corn at Stevie's head. Stevie ducked, and the corn struck the Principal in the face. A pickle then bounced off his forehead.

"This is only a test," Boris said, as Ernie's camera zoomed in for a close-up. "We've proven we can feed hungry kids. But as a candidate for …" Boris hesitated and for a moment a shadow settled over his face. "As a candidate for student council president and a Bendale student, I want to take it to the next level." He paused for dramatic effect. "I want to feed hungry kids all over the world!"

A milk carton hit the Principal in the back.

CHAPTER TWENTY-SIX

It had been a busy day, and it still wasn't over. Boris and I were pedaling hard toward the Munch Mart to see if we could secure more food for Operation Feed the World. I'd spent most of the day racing around the school hanging posters asking for food donations, and dodging the Principal and janitors angry about this morning's mess in the cafeteria. Boris did his share of dodging as well so he could make several impromptu speeches in classrooms. The negative reaction to Boris's speeches from a few teachers was disappointing, as was the detention for organizing the breakfast without the Principal's permission. We did raise two dollars, which Boris thought would be enough to buy a small bag of rice.

Boris and I agreed that a detention was a small price to pay for the opportunity to feed hungry kids, do a television interview and give Boris a chance to speak directly to the electorate. At the Munch Mart, Boris hopped off his bike and was inside before I had a chance to fasten my lock.

"The manager is in the back office," Boris called to me as I entered, and he began to weave between the fruits and vegetables. Boris raced past the dairy section and began to pound vigorously on a door.

It opened and a woman popped her head out.

"I told you, I'm —" Her voice softened when she noticed us. "Oh, sorry. I thought you were staff. Can I help you?"

"I think you can, my good friend," Boris said expansively.

"Great," she said.

"You are just the person I need."

"Wonderful. How can I help?"

"Do you agree that world hunger is a terrible thing?"

"I suppose."

"Would you like to help?"

"How?"

"Is there any chance we could have some food — anything you have extra, lying around, don't really need — to give to hungry kids? We wanna send food to the World Youth Hunger Conference. And do you have any large cardboard boxes we could have?"

"Umm, we might have a few boxes in the back," the manager said. "So this is a food drive?"

"Way more than that," Boris said. "We're using logistics — the coordinating of ... the moving of food ... What is it again, Adrian?"

"The coordination of a series of complicated tasks in the best way possible, which in this case means shipping food from here to hungry kids who live somewhere else."

The manager stared at us. "I suppose we can spare some food. We have some canned tomatoes. Would that help?"

"Perfect!" Boris said. "The kids could make spaghetti sauce."

"Not sure we have spaghetti to give you," the manager said.

Boris's face fell. "I'd hate to disappoint the hungry kids. Tough to eat spaghetti sauce without spaghetti."

The manager smiled. "Perhaps I can add a few bags."

Boris's face beamed gratitude. "You're the best. We also have some money to buy rice, and I'm doing TV interviews about this, and I'll be sure to mention the Munch Mart."

Now the manager looked even happier than Boris. They were two really delighted people. "That would be amazing. Thanks," she said.

"Can we come tomorrow for the tomatoes and spaghetti?" Boris said.

"I don't work tomorrow, but Mandy will be here."

"Not a problem. We'll deal with Mandy, then. And you have boxes, right?"

The manager nodded.

"Thanks again. You're awesome — and so's the Munch Mart," Boris said. He turned to me. "I'll meet you at the cash. I just want to grab something."

Boris came scurrying down the baking aisle and put a bag of marshmallows and a can of chocolate sauce — one of our favorite snacks — on the checkout counter. He added a bag of rice, too.

He handed the cashier a ten-dollar bill. "I got this," he said to me. "It's the last of the campaign money."

CHAPTER TWENTY-SEVEN

Boris and I got through the next day without a detention. We didn't have time to celebrate, however. Operation Feed the World was scheduled to start at precisely five o'clock. Boris had given me a list of supplies to bring to his house. It was difficult balancing them all as I rode over, but I managed. I had to wonder why I needed to bring a winter coat, a sleeping bag, a flashlight and potato chips.

After I'd tossed the first stone off the War Room window, Boris poked his head out the window and then shinnied down the tree. I stashed my stuff in the neighbor's shed, patted Chaz a few times, and we headed off to the Munch Mart.

"I have an appointment with Mandy," Boris said to a cashier.

"She's in produce," the cashier said.

Boris headed to the fruits and vegetables. "Are you Mandy?" he asked a teenager stacking lemons into a pyramid.

Both her arms were tattooed — a mermaid with long flowing hair graced her left, and Mandarin lettering her right. I had decided to take up Mandarin last summer, and while my progress has been slow, I believe a rough translation would be "World peace is awesome." A tie-dyed T-shirt featuring concentric rings of green and yellow extended to just above her belly button. A jade necklace, jeans and an assortment of facial and ear piercings completed her look. She was remarkably attractive. I immediately felt guilty and reminded myself that I hoped to be Frieda's boyfriend one day.

She pointed to another woman speaking into a phone. Boris headed over.

I paused to admire the mermaid.

"I believe you're Mandy," Boris said to the woman on the phone.

She hung up and put the phone in her pocket. "I am. Can I help you?"

"You sure can," Boris said. "For a start, where should we collect the tomatoes?"

"I'm sorry?"

Boris seemed somewhat taken aback. "This was all worked out with your boss, the manager."

"Sorry, she's not here. What is it you arranged? I'm in a bit of a hurry. We have to do a total inventory check tonight, plus restock the veggies."

Boris nodded sympathetically. "I've figured out a way to feed hungry kids around the world. Your manager said you had tomatoes and spaghetti for hungry kids, and to come today to get it. I did forget to ask one thing, though."

"What's that?"

"Would it be possible for you to drive the food somewhere? We're only talking five minutes." Boris's puppy-dog eyes would have broken a stone's heart.

Mandy grabbed her phone and tapped out a message. "Hold on a sec," she said in answer to Boris's continued puppy-dog-eyed request. Finally she put her phone away. "Okay. The manager told me to give you some tomatoes and spaghetti. Was she talking about the cans that were mislabeled? We were going to send them back to the warehouse."

"I guess so," Boris said. "Must be."

"Fine. How many do you want?"

"As many as you can spare," Boris said. "There are a lot of hungry kids to feed."

Mandy's eyebrows arched. She didn't have Boris's one-brow trick, but she did get them fairly high. "Okay. I suppose we can give you a few cans and a dozen bags of pasta."

"And the manager said you had boxes ..." The puppy-dog plea was still full on. I'd never seen him maintain it for so long. It had to be a record.

"Well ... I'm so busy right now. If I show you the tomatoes and spaghetti, could you box them yourselves?"

"No problem — and the boxes?"

"In the back."

"And the driver?"

"He should be here in half an hour or so. If it's only five minutes, and it's for charity ..."

"I don't suppose she could help us?" I asked, gesturing toward my mermaid-inked crush. "I don't want to make a mistake and take the wrong items."

She really was remarkably attractive — and I wanted another chance to study the Mandarin tattoo.

Mandy arched her eyebrows even higher this time. "May as well. It's not like she does any work around here.

177

Saves me the trouble of showing you where the food is. Hey, April?" she said loudly. "Can you take these boys to the shipping area and help them load some tomato cans and spaghetti into a box? Their school is having a food drive."

April threw a lemon at the pyramid and walked toward the back of the store. The lemons began to tumble to the floor, one by one. Mandy ran over. Boris signaled me to follow April, which I was more than willing to do. April proved to be a whiz with a forklift. She began loading two skids of canned tomatoes into three very large boxes. On top of the cans she loaded a skid of dried spaghetti. I guessed there were at least a thousand cans and three hundred bags of spaghetti.

Boris tossed the bag of rice in with the spaghetti.

"That's a lot of tomatoes," I said to April.

She yawned and parked the forklift.

Boris pulled an empty box, even larger than the other three, from the corner. "I bought a new marker for the job," Boris said, handing it to me, along with a piece of paper with his handwriting on it. "You write a bit neater than me. Could you copy the address from this paper onto each box?"

I wrote the addresses out quickly.

World Youth Hunger Conference
Wynchester Castle
184 Hollow Hedge Lane
Corktown

A touch of sadness washed over me. To see the faces on those hungry kids as we delivered the food would have been gratifying. It would have made everything Boris had gone through since the start of Operation S.O.S. worthwhile.

April closed the box tops with packing tape.

"Thanks for all your help," Boris said to her.

She shrugged.

"*Zài Jiàn,*" I said, which is "goodbye" in Mandarin.

She gave me a strange look and then sat down in a chair and closed her eyes. I didn't think it was possible to fall asleep so quickly.

The bay doors opened. A stocky man wearing a hard hat and blue overalls with the Munch Mart logo over his right breast hopped up the stairs and into the loading area. "Hi, April. You taking your break — again?" His laugh sounded like a machine gun.

April opened her eyes. She made a face, got up and walked slowly back into the store.

I was sad to see her go.

"Mandy sent me a text that there's a box for me to deliver, something about a charity?" he said.

"We need these delivered to a shipping company," Boris said, pointing to the four boxes.

"Where?" the driver said.

"It's not far — about a five-minute drive," Boris said. "But would it be a problem to drop me and Adrian off at my house first?" Boris said. "It's real close."

The driver shrugged. "Okay. Hurry it up, though."

"Don't forget the empty box," Boris reminded the driver. We re-entered the store through the plastic curtain.

"Thanks, Mandy," Boris yelled.

Mandy was counting egg cartons stacked on a skid. She waved her left hand over her head, her right index finger poking egg cartons all the while.

April was in the detergent section.

"*Zài Jiàn*," I said to her again.

Beautiful — yes.

Chatty — no.

I considered our age difference and realized it would never work out between us. Besides, my heart was pledged to Frieda.

Boris unchained our bikes and we rode around to the truck.

"Throw your bikes in the back and hop in next to me," the driver told us. Moments later we turned onto Boris's street.

"You can stop here," Boris said when the truck was still a few houses away.

"But your house is —"

"This is perfect," Boris said, cutting me off.

The driver stopped. "Can you wait for another minute?" Boris said. "I need to check something."

He shrugged and told Boris to hurry. We went to the back of the truck. Boris opened the door, climbed into the truck and handed me the bikes and Gordie.

"Can you put the bikes and Gordie in the shed, get your stuff and then meet me here?"

"Of course," I said. "But why meet back at the truck?"

"I'll explain it all in a minute," Boris said. "Trust me. But we gotta hurry before the driver takes off."

This was Boris at his finest: in charge, decisive, energetic — ready for greatness. I rolled the bikes to the shed, Gordie bumping along behind. Chaz sniffed me suspiciously and looked around for Boris. When he didn't see him, he whined a few times and lay down, his snout between his paws. He and Boris had become great pals lately. I stored the bikes and ran to the truck with my things.

Boris was talking to the driver. "I'll just close the back door for you," Boris said. "When I bang the side of the truck, you're good to go." He none too gently pulled me to the back door. He clambered into the truck and motioned for me to do the same.

"What are we doing?" I asked, but was immediately hushed up. I climbed in.

Boris pulled the rope and the door rolled down, plunging us into darkness. Then I heard two loud bangs, not unlike the sound of a hand slapping the side of a truck. The driver took that as the signal to go. The truck lurched, and I was sent sprawling into a box. Boris shone a flashlight in my eyes.

"Why are you lying down?" he asked.

"Why are we in the back of a moving truck?" I countered.

"I've arranged to meet Sandy when the food arrives at the conference," Boris said. "She said this story has a chance of going national."

"But why are we in the back of this truck?" I repeated.

Boris took a deep breath. "I had enough money in my Tiny Tots Savings Account to pay for shipping the food to the conference but not enough for bus tickets, and my parents said 'Absolutely no way' when I asked if they wanted to go to Corktown tomorrow."

We stared at each other.

"And I didn't think your parents would drive us," he said.

"I don't think they would either," I said.

"So I had to figure out a way for us to get to Corktown without paying," he said.

"We're going to Corktown?" I said.

"We have to be there to deliver the food and do the interview with Sandy," Boris said.

"But I didn't tell my parents I was going to Corktown," I said.

"I dealt with that. I sent an email to your mom saying that we had been invited to the conference, which is true. Ms. Crimpet invited us after the play. I said you needed to sleep over because my parents would want to leave early —"

"Your parents aren't driving us," I said.

"True, but if they were driving us we would have to leave early," he said.

I considered his explanation. "I think … that's a lie," I said, practically in shock.

"It's not a lie … more like not the entire truth."

"Well — it's not really honest."

He patted my shoulder. "I couldn't think of what else to say, and we really need to get to Corktown. It would've been way easier if we'd been on the final list for the conference, but we can't let that hold us back. You'll be home by tomorrow afternoon, I promise. Sandy said Ernie will give us a lift." He pulled out a box of Tic Tacs from his pocket and gave it a shake. "When our folks hear that we fed hungry kids from around the world, they won't be mad, or at least they won't be too mad."

Never mind our parents — I found *myself* getting mad. Boris has often told me I need to stand up for myself — and here I was being forced to do something I hadn't known about. "You didn't ask me. You lied to my parents. I wish you'd told me your entire plan before I got in the truck. I … I'd like to be able to decide things for myself." My voice quivered slightly. "Sometimes you make decisions without asking me, and … and … I don't really like that."

I had never been so forceful with Boris.

Boris lowered his flashlight. In a quiet voice, he said, "I didn't mean to. The driver will take you back if you want. You don't have to help anymore. You've done enough, and you're right. I didn't ask. Sometimes I get carried away, and I don't think about anything else. A real friend doesn't do that. Sorry, Adrian."

The truck turned a corner and we both fell against a box. Boris retrieved his flashlight.

"You didn't tell me how we're getting to Corktown," I said. "This truck is only going to the shipping company. They won't let us stay in the truck."

Boris pointed at the empty box.

"In there?" I gasped.

"It's the only way," he said. Boris held up a duffel bag. "I got all the supplies we'll need for the night, including salt-free cashews."

Salt-free cashews were my number-one favorite snack food.

"Will you promise to tell me what we're going to do from now on?" I said.

"Absolutely."

"And I mean the entire plan, not just bits and pieces — so I can decide whether I want to do it?"

Boris nodded emphatically.

"And maybe we can cut down on the number of suspensions and detentions?"

"I can't promise zero."

"That would be impossible, of course."

I extended my arm and he did the same.

With all the things Boris had done to organize Operation Feed the World, he still remembered to bring me salt-free cashews. It meant a lot. At the same time, I felt proud for standing up for myself. From now on, I knew we'd have a more honest, equal relationship.

Boris began to carve a hole in the side of the empty box for us to climb through.

CHAPTER TWENTY-EIGHT

My head banged into the side of the box and then off Boris's shoe before finally landing on a salami sandwich. I'll say this for Boris: he knows how to travel first-class in a box. Boris had packed snacks, board games, cards and a battery-operated lamp, and with the pillows, sleeping bags and my supplies, it was downright comfy. In a nod to Rule Three, he even brought carrot sticks and cucumber slices. Eventually, we began to tire, and then exhaustion set in. When I awoke, Boris was splayed out against the far wall, snoring away. I noticed the Tic Tacs on the floor and put them in my pocket for safekeeping. Without anything else to do, I turned on my tablet and began to write the day's entry for the blog.

The brakes began to squeal, and we slowed until we came to a complete stop. It had been stop-and-go for some time now. I heard a loud rattling sound, and the back door slid up. Boris's eyes popped open.

"What's this?" a man with a shrill voice demanded. "Take these away at once. Yes, this is Wynchester Castle, but this shipment is not authorized."

"This is the shipping address. Don't ask me."

"We have ambassadors, politicians and movie stars from around the world at this conference. You can't just drop off four huge boxes. It's a security issue."

I turned the tablet off. Boris slowly pulled duct tape away from the side of the box and pushed open the hole he'd cut out. We inched our way to the edge of the truck.

"They're arguing. We can make it. Come on," he whispered.

"I'm off-loading these boxes and there's nothing you can do to stop me, so point me to the delivery entrance or I drop them here at the front gates," the driver said.

We got down from the truck and made our getaway. We walked through a stone gate. Before us stood a castle — a real, live castle.

A sign over the front door proclaimed it the "Fourth Annual World Youth Hunger Conference." Boris barely hesitated. He marched up the cobblestone path. Up ahead stood an enormous doorway, at least ten feet high, each door a foot-and-a-half thick. He continued through it into the building, made a hard right, then another right and then continued straight ahead. His instincts proved spot-on. We'd had nowhere to pee except glass jars since last night, so a bathroom was a welcome sight.

We attended to our business promptly. A short walk took us to the main lobby, an impressive space with white marble flooring, a stuccoed ceiling with gold-leaf detailing and a series of spiral pillars. Two massive staircases at either end led to the second floor.

"We should check out the conference and find out where to direct the food," Boris said, checking his watch. "We have time to kill before Sandy and Ernie get here." A group of people were walking toward some doors. Boris fell in with them, and together we entered a sumptuous banquet hall with dozens of round tables scattered about and a head table at the far end with ten people or so. A multicolored banner over their heads proclaimed, "Take a Bite Out of Youth Hunger."

Boris pointed to a couple of empty seats near the front. We sat.

"Mushroom or cheese omelette?"

A tall, thin man dressed in a bright red jacket and black pants pointed to two silver serving trolleys. I was hungry, and breakfast seemed an excellent idea. I chose a cheese omelette, home fries and toast and helped myself to some tea.

"And for you, young man?" the waiter asked Boris.

"Sounds good," Boris said.

"Which one?" the waiter asked.

"Which one what?" Boris said. He held his plate out. The waiter served him both omelettes.

"Home fries?"

Boris just laughed. The waiter placed a few on his plate. Boris laughed again and kept his plate out. The waiter added a few more. Boris smiled. The waiter kept adding them until I feared they would tumble to the floor.

"Thanks." Boris sniffed his food with delicacy. "I feel guilty about eating, though," he said to the lady next to him.

"Youth hunger is a terrible thing," she said, turning with a smile to Boris. "So which school are you from?"

"We're from Bendale," Boris said.

The lady gave us both a dazzling smile. "That's

wonderful. It's really so wonderful to see young people getting involved. Inspiring," she said to a short, squat and very bald man with a scrunched-up face, bushy eyebrows and cold brown eyes.

He seemed unimpressed.

"Is your school making a presentation at the conference?" the lady asked.

Boris shrugged. "I'm not really sure. We weren't on the list. We brought food for the hungry kids," he said.

The man glared at us. The lady seemed uncertain about something. They began whispering to each other.

"Do you have invitations to attend the conference?" the lady asked abruptly.

I began to stutter.

"We don't have them with us," Boris said. "We have friends from school here. Ms. Crimpet didn't pick us." The lady stared at him. "But we weren't gonna let that stop us. We brought the canned tomatoes and spaghetti for the hungry kids — and the rice."

"We're here as … unofficial observers," I offered. "Boris is running for student council president and …" I thought it best to leave it at that.

"I've never heard of unofficial observers," the lady said. "This is the executive table, and you really need an invitation to attend the conference."

The man and the lady whispered to each other again. They got up and walked off. Then things got awkward. I heard a most unwelcome voice.

"What are you doing here, Snodski?" Robert said. "I saw you guys come in but couldn't believe you'd be so lame as to crash the conference. Ms. Crimpet will freak.

You'll be suspended for a hundred years if the Principal finds out."

Boris's expression was heroic. "I can't be worried about that when there are kids going hungry every day. That's why me and Adrian brought food, a ton of it."

"What are you talking about?" Robert said. "You brought food here? Where?"

"We shipped three big boxes full of canned tomatoes and pasta — and rice — from Bendale, using logistics," Boris said. "And after we deliver the food to the hungry kids, we have a television interview, and then we'll go home."

"Hungry kids? There are no hungry kids here," Robert said. "Are you the biggest doofuses ever? This is a conference, not a food bank."

It occurred to me that perhaps Robert had a point, possibly a major point. I had assumed Boris had done research and knew that bringing food was an important part of the conference. Robert's mocking expression suggested otherwise.

Robert began laughing. "You thought the World Youth Hunger Conference was a place where hungry kids come to get food? And I actually worried about you running for president? You're the saddest dudes in school — and maybe the dumbest. But I'll be nice 'cause you're so pathetic. I won't tell Crimpet. You gotta sneak outta here — real quick."

"There are no hungry kids at the conference?" Boris said, his voice thin.

Robert rolled his eyes. "This is a conference where rich people talk about hungry kids. Anyway, seriously, you need to make tracks and get going. If Crimpet sees you, you're cooked."

Suddenly, a shout rang out from the head table.

"How dare you!"

Two men stood and glared at each other.

"Where is my wife's ring, Mr. Ambassador?" a man in a blue suit raged.

"I do not know, Mr. Ambassador," a man in a brown suit replied.

"You insult me with your lies," Blue Suit said. "You were sitting next to my wife. The ring slipped off her finger because the home fries were greasy, and now it's gone. Only you were close enough to take it. I should have expected such treachery from you."

"I will not tolerate such an insult," Brown Suit said. "Apologize."

"I will not apologize to a thief."

"You — you dare to speak such lies?" Brown Suit sputtered. "There will be consequences."

"How dare you accuse me of lying?" Blue Suit said. "I will be making a phone call to my prime minister, requesting that he cancel the potluck lunch with your prime minister."

"You would cancel the annual potluck?" Brown Suit cried. "You're insane."

"You leave me no choice."

"Then we will cancel Skip-to-School Day," Brown Suit said.

Blue Suit seemed stunned by the idea. "Skip-to-School Day is my daughter's favorite day of the year," he said.

"I didn't cancel the potluck," Brown Suit said.

"Say goodbye to the Cherry Pie–Making Contest," Blue Suit said.

A tap on my shoulder interrupted my observation of the drama. Gazing down at Boris and me was a muscular man in a crisp black suit. He had an earphone stuffed into one ear and a rectangular silver badge embossed with the word "Security" pinned to his jacket. The lady and the bald man from earlier sat back down at our table, both smiling smugly. Robert stuck his tongue out at us.

"Can I speak to you in the hall, please?" the security guard said.

"We thought we'd stay for the presentations," I croaked.

"Now," the security guard said firmly.

I waited for Boris to make the call. I wondered if this was the time for Plan 3L, which would see us throw the toast in the air, crawl under two tables and then hightail it to the nearest exit.

Boris scrunched his nose, got up and followed the security guard.

I was at a loss. What was Boris doing? The guard would most certainly prevent us from meeting with Sandy and Ernie, and we still had to figure out what to do with the tomatoes and spaghetti — and the rice.

"Should we go with Plan 2X45?" I whispered. That required three shoulder rolls, a spin and a sprint to the nearest window.

I noticed a familiar head pop out from behind a plant and then disappear again. Was it a stress-induced delusion or the real Lynda Skittle? Then I remembered the list. She'd been selected as the third-grade rep.

Boris continued to march behind the security guard as if he hadn't heard me.

"What about Plan 2P17?"

Again, Boris didn't respond.

My mind whirled in desperation.

What was the plan?

What had happened to the B-Ster?

CHAPTER TWENTY-NINE

The guard opened the door and motioned us through. The two ambassadors were continuing their war of words, which had escalated to finger jabbing. Conference attendees began crowding around, presumably the better to hear their bitter exchange. Robert waved to us. The door closed.

Boris needed to make the call already.

"*What* is the plan?" I said, loudly this time.

"I don't know," he said unsteadily.

I couldn't have been more shocked if you had told me Euler's equation measuring spheres, $V - E + F = 2$, was wrong. We'd been chased too many times to count, and whether it was teachers, janitors, the Principal, parents, psychologists, firefighters or Italian tourists, Boris had never failed me. His escape plans did not always work, but they were always dramatic, imaginative, wild and — well — fun.

"We have to deliver the food — and meet with Sandy," I said.

I don't quite know what got into me. Call it inspiration if you like — or call it madness — but like at the wrap party when I charged after Boris's backpack, I sprang into action. I grabbed Boris by the collar and pulled him away from the security guard.

"Run," I screeched, knocking a sign over.

I felt a twinge of guilt when the security guard tumbled over the sign, but these were desperate times, and we needed to distance ourselves in a hurry. I had to hope Rule One justified my recklessness. I dragged Boris to the staircase at the far end of the lobby. Unfortunately, the security guard was back on his feet, and he had four fellow guards with him.

"What are we doing?" Boris said.

"Running up the stairs," I said.

"Why?"

"To get away."

"But we can't get away."

I knew the situation looked bleak. Negativity wouldn't help, though. I led him to the third floor.

"Stop at once," a voice commanded. "You cannot escape."

"He's right," Boris said.

"This way," I said, running toward the staircase at the other end leading back to the lobby. "What's gotten into you?" I said to Boris. "We need a plan — and quick!"

We headed down the stairs.

"My plans never work," he said. "Think of the swings. I was tied upside down and kids threw pinecones at my head."

"But the little kids got the swings at recess."

"What about now? I really thought there'd be hungry kids here."

I jumped the last few stairs. We were back at the lobby. It occurred to me that we hadn't made much progress, but in my defence, I wasn't used to making these types of decisions. "They'll never expect the double-back trick," I said.

The double-back was a Snodbuckle favorite.

"We're going in circles," Boris said.

I tugged on his shirt and we sprinted across the lobby and back to the first staircase. In short order I saw that I'd overestimated the double-back. The security guards were charging after us.

"Can we stop running?" Boris said.

I almost did. Boris Snodbuckle wanted to quit? I figured he was just disoriented from spending so much time in a cardboard box.

"Time for Plan B," I said.

If there was ever a time for a Plan B, it was now, particularly as I didn't have a Plan A. We went up to the landing on the second floor again. This time I spotted a set of very large bay windows and next to it a fire hose unit.

"Open those windows," I ordered as we ran over.

Boris gave me a quizzical look but did as I asked. "Now what?" he said.

I quickly estimated the distance to the ground, measured out the fire hose and hastily fashioned a harness. "We have to go with Plan Triple-S24, Second Variation," I said. "It's our only chance."

The security guards had reached the top of the stairs.

"Forget it, Adrian. There's no point," Boris said.

I put the harness around us and hustled Boris onto the window ledge.

"Please get down," a security guard yelled.

"Jump," I said.

Boris stared back blankly.

Boris's disoriented brain obviously made it impossible for him to think straight. I took a deep breath, prayed my calculations were correct and, grabbing Boris by the shoulders, hurled us out the window. Sheer terror took away any sensation of falling.

My feet had almost touched the ground when we were jerked back up. We tumbled out of the harness into a recently planted flower bed that was soft and mulchy.

"Are you boys crazy?" a security guard yelled at us from the window above.

"Yes," I said, "and sorry about the flowers."

I pulled Boris to his feet and we set off toward the rear of the building. An open side door caught my eye. As much as Boris loved the double-back, he absolutely adored the double-double-back. I motioned for Boris to go inside.

Boris looked exhausted as I pushed him through the doorway. "Adrian, I shipped three boxes of food to a conference about hungry kids — that has no hungry kids! I used up all the money I've saved since kindergarten. I even broke the Code. I lied to your parents about what we were doing — and I think I sorta lied to Mandy at the Munch Mart by not really telling her what her manager said. I knew her manager never wanted us to have all that food." He took a deep breath. "We did all this for nothing, and I'm tired of things never working out — never — and of kids putting me down all the time ... and the jokes about my name ... and no matter what I do, all I ever get are detentions and suspensions."

"I agree the detentions can be —"

Boris refused to be mollified.

"My parents are always mad at me, and your parents are always mad at me — and the Principal and all the teachers are always mad at me ..."

"Not Ms. Crimpet."

"Okay. Not her, but everyone else! And she will be now that we're going to be arrested by security guards and tossed out of the conference. And Sandy's gonna be mad, too." He reached into his pockets and threw up his hands. "Great. I even lost Ernie's Tic Tacs."

I pulled them from my pocket.

"Well, I misplaced them, so ... thanks. At least I didn't mess that up," Boris said. He crossed his arms. "The worst part is I get you in trouble all the time. You shouldn't hang out with me. I always ruin things for you. I bet you'd have won the Science Fair if I hadn't soaked the Principal. I think he voted against you because of me."

"It just wasn't my year," I said. "I didn't really have much time to prepare —"

"I try, but things never work the way I expect," Boris continued in the same bitter tone. "You gotta admit that. Think about the breakfast — more like a food fight."

"I blame the raccoons," I said.

"Can you honestly say I have a chance of winning the election against Robert Pinsent, especially when people find out about this? I can hear Pinsent now: 'Buckle Butt, why'd you send spaghetti and tomatoes to the middle of nowhere? Is it 'cause you're stupid or just really stupid?'" Boris hung his head. "Maybe it's the second one," he murmured.

We remained silent, the two of us, deep in thought. My inability to read minds made it difficult for me to know what Boris was thinking. If I had to guess, I'd say the B-Ster was down, and at a most inconvenient time.

Because he had never let the suspensions and the detentions and the name-calling and the ... other minor setbacks bother him before, it had never occurred to me that Boris would become discouraged by any of it. Clearly, I was wrong. I felt awful. A first-rate sidekick should know better. Boris was born with extraordinary talents and gifts, and he usually had the confidence of ten kids, but even he needs to hear an encouraging word on occasion.

"If it wasn't for Boris Snodbuckle, what would I have done these past seven years?" I began. "I would never have figured out how long pizza slices can stick to the cafeteria doors or ... I mean ... You're the B-Ster, and so what if all of your plans don't work out? In the end, they do because ... because every operation is an adventure. Without you, I'd be sitting in my bedroom reading *Science* magazine all day and, well, I wouldn't have even joined Science Club without you ... Remember in fifth grade when we made Velcro suits and attached ourselves to the ceiling in the Principal's office to test out a spy idea? We were there for a whole hour before the Principal saw us."

Boris looked at me with sad eyes. "Yeah. And we couldn't get down, so the Principal had to call the janitors, and we got suspended."

My words tumbled out.

"But it was one of the greatest days of my life. It was ... fun. Maybe the Velcro was too strong. But we learned something, and next time we won't make the same mistake. Sure, maybe you picked the wrong place to send the spagetthi and tomatoes ... and rice. Who cares? We still have the food. All we need to do is figure out where to send it. We know there are hungry kids out there. Let's find them. And okay, you broke the Code. You'll apologize like you said, and you'll make sure not to do it again. You're not perfect — and you don't have to be. But you're the B-Ster, and you can't stop being him. Let's finish Operation Feed the World, do the interview with Sandy and then win that election."

"We can't win," he said. "It's over."

"We'll know that when the votes have been counted — not before."

"I sent food to a conference that doesn't need food."

"You tried to help. Wasn't that what you really wanted to do? And no election's gonna change that."

Boris didn't answer for the longest time. "I guess we proved we could move food a long way."

"That's the B-Ster spirit," I exclaimed. "You can't give up now. You owe it to Bendale, to the kids who have trouble making friends, to the kids who get bullied ... and get balls thrown at their heads in dodgeball ... and to the kids who get pulled or don't get invited to parties ..."

I was forced to stop talking momentarily owing to the inconvenient tears rolling down my cheeks. "You owe it to me — I mean them, to Bendale students ... to show them that the most popular kid in school can't fake his way into being student council president — not without a fight, anyway. We need someone who cares enough to try to stop him. We need Boris Snodbuckle if we want Bendale to become a great school — for all of us."

Boris's eyes flashed. "If Robert Pinsent wins, I bet the first thing he'll do is take the swings away from the primaries."

"We can't let that happen."

"And it'll be dodgeball every day."

"I have no doubt."

"And the Principal will have indoor recess every chance he gets."

"Of course he will!"

"And the Wedgie War will never end."

"For sure."

Boris straightened his shoulders. "What time you got?"

"It's close to ten o'clock."

"We have to meet Sandy in fifteen minutes."

"But how? I'm out of ideas, and the security guards are looking for us outside."

"We attack from the inside. Come on." He waved me forward.

Boris was back!

I followed happily. Together we continued down the narrow corridor. It grew darker and darker until I could barely see where I was going.

"Ooof," I gasped. The echo drifted down the hall.

In the darkness, I had managed to walk into something very hard. I felt around briefly until a terrible smell assaulted my nose. I had walked into a couple of garbage bins. I rubbed my knee and was about to complain about the pain to Boris when the overhead lights snapped on. Muffled voices could be heard from the other end of the corridor. We dropped to the ground and scampered behind the garbage bins.

"They're coming," I whispered. "They'll find us here. I blew it. I shouldn't have made us come back in. Sorry, Boris."

"You didn't blow anything," Boris said. The voices got louder. He swung open the lid to a garbage bin. "You take the other one," he said, and he began to climb inside.

Boris and I once spent an afternoon in the school's garbage bin during a game of hide-and-seek, so I have experience. The smell reminded me of a baby's dirty diaper soaked in grease, sprinkled with tuna fish juice and baked in moldy cheddar cheese.

We won that hide-and-seek game, by the way.

"MacTavish is so lame," I heard someone nearby say. "He's got me working a double shift tomorrow."

"He gives the best shifts to Virgil and Corey. Totally bogus."

I covered my head with a bag. The lid swung open. Something wet oozed onto my head.

The lid closed. I forced myself to remain still, no easy task when cold, wet garbage is dripping down your back. The lid opened again, and once more I had to endure a garbage shower. I heard the lid to Boris's bin open as well.

"I'm gonna tell MacTavish what I think of him."

"Yeah, right, tough guy."

"You watch me."

"I will."

"Fine."

"Fine."

The debate faded away until finally all was quiet. I didn't hear Boris move. I figured he wanted me to hold tight until he was sure they'd gone. I leaned back into something squishy and closed my eyes. All that running had tired me out.

CHAPTER THIRTY

The horrific smell aside, soft garbage is not unpleasant to lie in, and I found myself getting rather sleepy. I think I even drifted off a bit, until a banging roused me from my slumber.

"Get out!"

The voice sounded familiar, but it was definitely female and very high-pitched.

I lifted the lid tentatively.

Boris was standing in his bin. I figured that meant the coast was clear, and I stood also. Bits of omelette clung to Boris's shirt. Bread crumbs covered his hair. His shoulders were stained brown — my guess was tea.

Lynda Skittle stared up at me. "Why are you in the garbage?" she said.

"We were about to get caught and this was the only place to hide," I said. "How'd you find us?"

"I followed you," she said. "Why'd you jump out the window?"

"To escape from the security guards," I said. "How'd you find us after we landed in the flower bed?"

"The guards ran back downstairs and I climbed down the fire hose," she said.

"You're good at following people," I said.

"You're both nutsos," she said. Lynda reached into her pocket. "Anyway, you guys gotta help me. I'm gonna get in huge trouble, and I know you guys know all about trouble."

She held up an enormous diamond ring.

"The ring!" I exclaimed. "Where'd you find it?"

"Those ambassadummies were so busy yelling at each other they didn't notice it fell off the table and rolled under the stage. I was under there and found it. But Ms. Crimpet told me not to leave the table where we were sitting. But we were way in the back and I couldn't hear what was going on. I sneaked under the stage and hid, and I found lots of other cool stuff, including this."

She dug in her other pocket and pulled out what looked like a wooden handle. She hit a button and a comb popped out.

"That is kinda cool," Boris said.

"Crimpet will be totally mad when she finds out I went under the stage, and she'll be double mad when she finds out I followed you guys around, and my parents will be crazy mad if I get another detention," she said. "One more detention and they won't let me have a sleepover for my birthday."

She flung her little fists in the air and stomped her feet in frustration.

"Ms. Crimpet is nice. We'll talk to her," I said. "And I truly feel your pain about the detentions."

"And we can help you with the ring," Boris said.

"Really!" Lynda squealed with delight.

"Not a problem," Boris said, as he wiped some egg yolk off his cheek and climbed out of his bin.

I climbed out also.

"Can I have it?" Boris asked.

He held out his baby finger and Lynda slid it on.

"I have an idea," Boris said. "If it works, no one will know that you found the ring under the stage, which means Ms. Crimpet won't know you snuck off."

"Go for it, Snodbuckle," Lynda said.

"Let's do it," I said.

"Hold on, Adrian. Remember you wanted to know my plans so you could decide whether to come or not?" he said to me.

"We have to act fast," I said. "Sandy's going to leave if she doesn't see us. I trust you."

Boris extended his arms. Lynda and I took hold in a group Roman handshake.

"Operation Diamondback begins," Boris said. "What're your code names?"

"I'd like to go with Dark Night," I said.

"I'm Black Storm," Lynda said.

"Sounds good. I'll be Invisible Shadow," he said.

Boris lowered himself into a deep squat, arms parallel to the floor. He looked right, then left, then right, then left.

"This way," he whispered.

He led us down the hall. His directional hunch paid off because we ended up in front of a door that led to a staircase, which then led to another staircase, which finally took us to a huge kitchen. After a difficult conversation with a chef, who had trouble understanding why Boris and I were covered in food, we ended up back in the banquet hall.

It was mostly empty by this time, apart from a large crowd still gathered near the head table. Ernie had his camera on his shoulder.

"Sandy, sorry we're late," Boris called out.

I tossed Ernie the Tic Tacs.

Robert stared at us, wide-eyed and pale. Off to the side, looking none too happy, stood Ms. Crimpet.

"Boris? Adrian? I don't understand. You missed the bus," Ms. Crimpet said.

"That's why we took the truck," Boris said.

Ms. Crimpet scratched her head.

Sandy sniffed the air. "I thought you were sending food to hungry kids, not wearing it," she said.

Boris laughed. "It's a long story. Is Ernie filming?"

"Not yet," Sandy said.

"He should. This is gonna be a big story," Boris said.

Sandy yawned. "I didn't know it was such a long drive."

"Just roll the camera," Boris said. "You won't be disappointed." He cuffed my arm. "C'mon, Dark Night."

"Who's Dark Night?" Ms. Crimpet said.

"I'm with you, Invisible Shadow," I said.

"Invisible what?" Robert said.

"Your people cannot live without our jams and marmalades," Blue Suit thundered.

"I hope you enjoy the Spring Fling Rose Festival without our shipment of roses," Brown Suit answered.

"My nation will continue to fling in the spring, roses or not," Blue Suit said.

"Fine."

"Fine."

"Great."

"Great."

Boris elbowed me in the side. "Tell them, Dark Night," he said.

"We found the ring," I shouted, holding Boris's hand over his head.

My declaration was not heard.

"Maybe *you* should try, Black Storm," Boris said.

"The ring is on his finger!" Lynda cried out.

The two ambassadors turned in unison.

"We found the ring in the garbage, Adrian and I," Boris said. "A waiter must've scooped the ring up when he was clearing the dishes."

Lynda looked up at Boris with thanks sparkling in her eyes. "Your hair isn't puffy like Pinsent's — but I like you more," she said.

"I have wronged you, my dear and oldest friend," Blue Suit said to Brown Suit. "To think I accused you of stealing when we went to grade school together, and university together, and my daughter married your son, and we take summer holidays together and live next door to each other. Please accept my apology."

Brown Suit proved a forgiving sort. "No need to say sorry. I understand and respect your profound love for your wife. Dear friend, let us not speak of this again. I look forward to receiving your letter of apology."

"I believe friends like us do not need to be so formal. My apology is heartfelt and sincere, and we can leave this unpleasantness behind us forever," Blue Suit said.

"I agree we should not dwell on such a terrible matter, but it's easy to say sorry. A real apology must be written," Brown Suit said.

Their faces hardened.

"Do you want your ring back or what?" Lynda asked Blue Suit.

Their faces softened.

"Thank you, my dear young lady, and thank you, young man, for finding it," Blue Suit's wife said to Boris. "I'm so grateful." Her nose wrinkled. A young woman took the ring from Boris with a tissue. "Please clean that, dear," Blue Suit's wife said to the young woman, "very well."

"Yes, ma'am," the young woman said, bowing slightly.

"I am amazed at your courage," Blue Suit said to Boris. He looked us over. "To have gotten so, ahem, involved with the garbage must have been ... difficult."

"It's no big deal for us. We're used to it. And it wasn't just me. I couldn't have done it without Adrian — and Lynda helped us ... get back to the banquet hall," Boris said. He took a sniff in the air and turned to Ms. Crimpet. "I gotta say, we could use my Science Fair exhibit about now. We really need to clean up."

"And you shall," Blue Suit said. "Immediately. You three will be my guests at the conference. My staff will take you to wash, and then I insist you visit us in our hotel suite, so my wife and I can hear the story about how you found our precious ring. It's immeasurably valuable, and it has been in my family for generations."

"Sounds great," Boris said. "I don't suppose you could help us send some tomato cans and spaghetti and rice to hungry kids? I have three large boxes of food sitting outside the gate."

"What a wonderful boy," Blue Suit's wife said. "He even brought food for hungry children to the conference. I'll take care of it personally." She called to her staff. The young woman holding the ring came to her. She whispered something in her ear.

"Yes, ma'am. I'll arrange for the food to be delivered to a lunch program for students," the young woman said.

"You can leave the empty box — that's got our stuff in it," I mentioned to the young woman.

"Now, please follow me," Blue Suit said, "and we can get you and your friend ... Dark Night ... cleaned up."

Brown Suit and his wife joined us. "I must insist that these boys and this adorable young lady be our guests," Brown Suit said. "Our country is famous for its hospitality and magnificent food. Please, come with us so we can thank you properly. You are true heroes — peacemakers."

I was dying to get to a computer to update the Feed the World blog. Boris had done it! He'd gotten Lynda out of trouble, and he'd gotten food to hungry kids. He would return to Bendale a hero. I also held out the faint hope that maybe Frieda would learn of my role in this adventure and be impressed.

"So please come with us," Brown Suit continued. "My friend will be too busy writing his apology letter."

"That will not take much time since it's so unnecessary," Blue Suit said.

"The Principal sometimes makes me write apologies," Boris said. "It's always a ton of work, and in the end the teachers are still mad at me. If you're really sorry, then you should just say it. Who needs a letter?"

"I hate apology letters," Lynda said. "They make my hand hurt."

Brown Suit pressed his hands together and bowed his head to Boris and Lynda. "I will accept the wise advice of our little heroes," he said, extending a hand to Blue Suit. "I accept your apology, even though it's not in writing."

"And I again offer an apology, which is really all you need to say when you're sorry."

Blue Suit's wife took Boris by the elbow. "Please come and be our guest."

"I believe he wants to be our guest," Brown Suit's wife said.

Their faces hardened.

"There's plenty of us to go around," Boris said. "You can guest us all."

"Such wisdom," Blue Suit said.

"He has both courage and intelligence," Brown Suit said.

"Excuse me for just a moment," Ms. Crimpet said. "These two boys are my students. Boris, Adrian — can you explain to me why you missed the bus?"

"We didn't miss the bus. We weren't invited," Boris said. "But Dark Night, or I mean Adrian, and I collected food for hungry kids. I really thought there'd be hungry kids at the conference. But when we found the ring, I figured these people could help deliver the food where it needed to go, since they were at the head table and look very important."

The two ambassadors puffed out their chests and nodded gravely.

"But I don't understand," Ms. Crimpet said. "You *were* invited. Both of you."

"Our names weren't on the list," I said.

"Robert, I gave you the list to hang on the bulletin board," Ms. Crimpet said. "What happened?"

Robert flashed his pearly white teeth angelically.

"I knew it," Lynda said. "You're a total lying liar, and it's your fault the Wedgie War keeps going."

"Robert Pinsent, I think you and I need to have a chat. Now!" Ms. Crimpet said to him very firmly.

Robert's face had lost most of its color.

"Wouldn't it be marvelous to have these nice people make a presentation to the conference?" Brown Suit's wife said. "Their story is so inspiring. Such devotion to the cause."

"A fantastic idea," Blue Suit's wife said.

The idea of speaking to the entire conference terrified me. There were hundreds of people.

"No problem," Boris said. "Tell us when and where."

"You got PowerPoint?" Lynda said, tossing a couple pieces of bubblegum in her mouth.

"We'll do the interview later once you've had a chance to clean up," Sandy said to Boris.

Boris flashed a thumbs-up.

"Follow me," Blue Suit said.

"I'll lead the way," Brown Suit said.

We followed them to the main doors.

"The most incredible series of events has just unfolded," Sandy said, turning to face Ernie's camera. "Three Bendale students, Boris Snodbuckle, the Skittle and Boris's friend, have stopped two countries from almost declaring war on each other, and they've also helped feed a lot of hungry kids. That's right. They stopped a war and fed hungry children. This amazing story happened this morning at the Fourth Annual World Youth Hunger Conference in Corktown."

PART VII

Operation
Beat His Speech

CHAPTER THIRTY-ONE

I found Boris reading some papers under the maple tree by the parking lot. Hard to believe only five days had passed since the World Youth Hunger Conference. Sandy's report had gone viral, beyond anything we could've imagined. Boris and I had been on television and interviewed by dozens of newspapers. Even better, and maybe as a result of that, Boris was now sitting at 12 percent in the Bendale presidential poll, with Robert hovering down around 70 percent. That left 18 percent of the voters undecided. I'd been up most of the night crunching the numbers, and I was excited to discuss it with him.

Boris wouldn't win, but he could get over 20 percent of the votes — maybe even more!

And given where he'd been in my last poll, that represented a minor miracle.

"Did you see the latest figures?" I asked him. "I emailed them to you last night."

"Sorry, Adrian. I was on the phone with Blue Suit's wife, the lady from the conference. She wants me to come to another conference in Paris, France, this summer," he said. "Brown Suit's wife wants me to come to London, England. Now they're in an argument about it ..."

"That's amazing," I said. "You must be very excited about a trip overseas."

He snatched some grass and tossed it in the air. "Not really. I told them I want to spend my time getting food for hungry kids, not talking about it. It was nice of them to offer, though."

"Okay. So you're at twelve percent in the polls," I said, "and according to my projections, you could end up with as much as twenty percent of the vote."

Boris sat up straight. "That really is amazing. For a long time there I thought I wouldn't get any votes."

"You knew you'd always get one!"

Boris waved me off. "You know what I mean."

I joined him on the ground. It was nice to relax after such a hectic few days.

"How are you liking your speech?" I asked.

Boris had been struggling with it. Ms. Crimpet had organized an assembly for this afternoon. The candidates for student council from each grade would have three minutes to address the student body, a last chance for the voters to judge the candidates before the election tomorrow.

He made a sour face. "I hate it," he said, handing me the sheets of paper. "It's not working for me. I've rewritten it about a hundred times."

I'd heard the speech. It was interesting, funny and powerful, and yet I understood what Boris meant. Something was missing. Something wasn't right.

And then I knew.

The Snodbuckle magic — the heart — the soul.

Boris had rewritten this speech so often the best part of it was gone — the B-Ster part.

A relaxing lie-down in the grass would have to wait. My sidekick duties beckoned.

I ripped the pages in half and crumpled them up.

"What are you doing?" Boris exclaimed. He reached for the ball of paper.

I held it firmly in my hand. "The problem with this speech is … it's not you. Speak from the heart. Speak your mind. Don't read a script. Tell everyone why you're running. Tell them what you believe in. It's time for One Hundred Percent Snodbuckle."

He gave me a double eyebrow flick. "That's a lot of Snodbuckle," he said.

"Bendale needs all of it," I said.

To state the obvious, we grasped forearms.

"You're right, Adrian. I'm going to just talk to them. If I can't think of anything to say, then I don't deserve their votes. It's gotta come from the heart, or not at all. Thanks. I can always count on you."

I turned away briefly, overcome with emotion. Boris could always count on me, but to hear him say it …

"Why're you sitting there like lumps?"

Lynda Skittle and her own faithful sidekick, Maggie, had come to pay us a visit.

"What should we be doing?" Boris said.

"You should be doing election stuff. Are you napping? Robert's giving out free pancakes in the caf."

Boris elbowed me. "I could go for a pancake," he said.

"You can't eat Robert's gross pancakes," Lynda yelled. "He's the enemy."

"He's not an enemy," Boris said kindly.

"He thinks you're the enemy," Lynda said. "He said you're stupid and you can't read and you're a liar." She looked at me. "And Michael says you're a doofus."

Maggie whispered something in Lynda's ear. "Thanks, Maggs. Robert also said you'll steal student council money because you stole Hurley's red notebook," she growled.

"He didn't steal that notebook," I said.

"So do something," Lynda pleaded to Boris. "You gotta say stuff about Robert or everyone will vote for him. Tell how he didn't do anything to stop the Wedgie War, how he lied about the swings, took credit for the Valley and tried to keep you from going to the conference — he lied about everything!"

She leaped to her feet, eyes ablaze, fists clenched, her skirt swaying gently in the breeze.

"I didn't help you just to get your vote. And you shouldn't vote for me just because you think I'll win. Lynda, would you be happy if I acted like Robert?" Boris said quietly.

Lynda slowly opened her fists. She lowered her gaze to the ground and kicked at the grass. "Dunno … maybe not."

"Would you feel good if I won the election because I said bad things about other people?"

She shrugged.

"Is that the way you want me to win the election?"

Lynda stuck her bottom jaw out and crossed her arms. "Guess not."

Brandon cleared his throat. He'd joined us beneath the maple tree.

Boris and I were not used to so many visitors at recess.

"Um, hi," Brandon said.

"What's up?" Boris said.

"I just wanted to ask if you'd seen … If you knew what Robert's been saying about you," Brandon said.

"I heard a few things," Boris said.

"I told him," Lynda said, "and he won't do anything."

"I heard him say you didn't sleep overnight in the Valley," Brandon said. "That you only pretended to, and then you showed up after it was all over."

"That's not right," I said. "I can't believe what's coming out of his mouth. Boris, you have to do something. These stories could change the polls."

Boris could dip below 10 percent if this stuff caught on!

Boris put his hands in his lap.

"Brandon, you can believe what you want. I can't do anything about that. The Valley didn't get destroyed, so does it really matter who slept there and who brought everyone to the protest?" Boris said.

Brandon's eyes darkened. "It matters because the environment isn't something you should protect just to be popular …" He left off and looked out into the parking lot.

Frieda pushed past him.

Our quiet recess had turned into quite a party.

"You better make a killer speech this afternoon, Snodbuckle, or Pinsent will win," she said.

"I'm going to try my best," Boris said.

"Try! You can't try — you have to do. That self-centered jerk will ruin this school. I don't trust him ..." Frieda broke off and turned to me. "Can't you write him a great speech? You're good with words and ... smart."

I had no time to process that comment.

The first bell rang. Recess was almost over.

"I guess we won't be getting those pancakes," Boris joked.

"Don't say I didn't warn you," Frieda said. "Use every argument and don't pull any punches."

"Yeah, punches!" Lynda said.

Frieda wasn't done. "Robert wants to make you look like a dweeb — and he's doing it. You have to tell everyone what kind of person he is. Tell them how he got Henson to trip you in *The Lion King*. It was on purpose. I saw it. Tell them that Robert and his friends make people nervous, and they make fun of you if you do well on a test. Tell them a kid who scares people and is a bully shouldn't be on the council. They should vote for someone who wants to *help* ..."

She was breathing heavily. I had never heard her so impassioned.

I desperately wanted to mention the Science Fair. Frieda had been humiliated by her second-place finish, but the Code forced me to keep my mouth shut.

Stevie and Jonah came running over.

"You still running for president?" Stevie said.

Boris nodded.

"Told ya," Jonah said.

"I knew it anyway," Stevie said.

"Did not. You said he chickened out," Jonah said.

"No way," Stevie said.

"Yes way," Jonah said.

This could go on for a while. The second bell was going to ring soon, and we had to get to class. "Yes, Boris is still running for student council president," I said.

Stevie held a hand up to me. "Duh! I just said that. Anyway, Boris, we wanted to tell you something. We know you didn't throw the script at Mr. Hurley during rehearsal. Do you remember? Hurley freaked on you — but I know you didn't do it."

"I'm the one who told you," Jonah said.

"Did not."

"Did too."

I could see where this was going.

"How do you know who threw the script?" I jumped in.

"Because I saw it," Stevie said.

"Because I saw it," Jonah said.

"Then why didn't you say anything?" I said.

Stevie and Jonah stared at me like I was crazy.

"I'll tell you who it was as long as you promise never to say I told you," Stevie said. "You gotta promise."

"You don't have to tell me," Boris said.

"But I want to. It'll help you win the election," Stevie said.

"Shhh," Jonah said. "You'll give it away. He hasn't promised."

"Okay," Boris said. "I promise."

Stevie and Jonah exchanged a look. Jonah nodded.

"Pinsent did it," Stevie said. "Everyone knows he did it. Half the *Lion King* cast saw him do it."

I was deeply disappointed. Did anyone at Bendale have courage?

"Don't worry about it," Boris said. "I ... I don't blame you. You couldn't do anything — not with Robert and his crew there. So forget about it."

"And Pinsent put Hurley's red notebook in Boris's backpack," Jonah whispered. "I saw him do it."

"You gotta use this to wreck Robert in the speeches — in front of the whole school," Stevie said. "Tell everyone that he lied to Hurley. You'll win for sure."

We all looked at Boris.

Boris had all the dirt on Robert he'd ever need — a lifetime of dirt.

"Thanks, guys," Boris said. "I'll ... think about it, and I guess I'll see you later, after the speeches."

Frieda crinkled her nose. "He's not going to do it. I can tell." She spun on her heels and left.

"Good luck with the speech," Brandon said. He left, too.

"You're nuts," Stevie said to Boris. "You can totally bring Pinsent down."

"And stupid Michael Beverley," Jonah said.

"And Wong, Henson and Daniels," Stevie said.

"Thanks for telling me," Boris said. "That took a lot of guts."

"Race ya to the doors," Stevie said to Jonah. He ran off.

"Totally unfair," Jonah cried, setting off after him. "This doesn't count. No way."

"Yes way," Stevie said.

"No way," Jonah said.

"C'mon, Maggs," Lynda said. "Let's grab a slide before we gotta go in."

She and Maggie slipped away to the equipment.

"Got your code name?" Boris said to me.

"What for?"

He grinned. "Operation Beat His Speech."

"Are you going to use anything you just learned about Robert?" I said

"No, that would be tattling. But I'm not giving up."

The B-Ster give up in the face of overwhelming odds? Preposterous.

I thought about my code name for a moment. "Winston Churchill was prime minister of England during World War Two and a famous speech maker. People used to think he looked like his bulldog, so I'll go with Bulldog."

"Sounds cool, Bulldog. I'm going with Wet Wipes," Boris said. He pointed to the school. "We should try to make it on time once this year."

Wet Wipes? I confess I didn't understand his code name.

Boris clapped me on the back as we walked. "We've done a lot since Operation S.O.S. started. Couldn't have done it without ya, Bulldog."

"A pleasure to serve, Wet Wipes."

Wet Wipes?

Why would he choose that name? I sensed a hidden meaning. But what?

To clean stuff? To clean a mess?

Boris held the door open and I went into the school.

Wet Wipes — the perfect code name for Operation Beat His Speech.

I'd figured it out.

Robert was the mess — and he needed to be cleaned up!

CHAPTER THIRTY-TWO

The entire school was packed into the gym for the student council speeches. Mr. Hurley held his hand up for quiet. He'd taken this as an opportunity to present Robert with the Artistic Bravery Award for finding his red notebook.

"In the immortal words of Genghis Khan, as he said goodbye to Flipity-Dipity, 'May your carrots be orange and your tail be fluffy.'"

Mr. Hurley clasped his hands over his head. "And I'll see you all in September when *Genghis Khan and Flipity-Dipity Rabbit — The Musical* opens at Brenda's Café!"

The Principal took the mic from Mr. Hurley, cast a raised eyebrow his way, cleared his throat and waved the student council candidates onstage. The number of candidates was disappointing. Only kids in fourth grade and above could run for a spot on student council. And only students in seventh grade could run for president of the council. Fourth grade had two candidates, fifth and sixth grade only one each — and two from seventh grade, Boris and Robert, who were running for president.

The Principal called up the two kids from fifth and sixth grade.

"Is there anyone else out there in fifth or sixth grade

who wants to run for student council?" the Principal asked. "Anyone?"

Evidently not.

The Principal puffed out his cheeks. "In that case, let me introduce your fifth-grade and sixth-grade student council reps."

The two kids waved.

The Principal pointed to the floor, and they rejoined their friends.

"Next, let's hear from the fourth-grade candidates," the Principal said.

I didn't listen too closely. Only fourth graders vote for the fourth-grade rep. No one else listened much either. Ms. Crimpet and the Principal tried to shush everyone. Mr. Grisham talked on his phone. Mr. Hurley hummed a song to himself.

The students only got louder.

I began to worry about Boris's speech. Would anyone be able to hear it?

"And that's why I think it'll be a great year!" the second fourth-grade candidate said in closing.

"Thank you," the Principal said, taking the mic from her. "Can I have the two candidates for president — Robert Pinsent and Boris Snodbuckle." The gym quieted slightly. "Let's all pay attention, please," the Principal continued. "Every student has a vote for president."

The Principal gave Robert the mic. "Why don't you go first?" he said.

Robert ran a hand through his hair a couple of times, gave his head a shake, grinned, ran his hand through his hair a few more times — and stepped forward.

"Go for it, Valley Monster," Michael called out.

Robert held his hand up for quiet. "'Sup, Bendale. We ready to crush it next year?"

"Big time, bro. Big time," Michael said.

"Well, I'm ready to crush it next year for sure — totally." He ran a hand through his hair. "You guys really want a Snodbuckley president? Seriously? No way you should vote for Snodbuckle. His name is Snodbuckle! He ruins everything. Think about the play when he knocked over the zebra, and I didn't want to say anything, but everyone knows that he stole Mr. Hurley's red notebook. I believe in being honest, and stealing isn't right. What about the fact he threw water over everyone at the Science Fair, which I won by the way, and he caused a food fight in the cafeteria. I went to his breakfast. He served corn. You guys like corn for breakfast? I served pancakes this morning. That's the difference between us. I serve pancakes, and he gives you corn. He's a joke. When I'm president, I'm going to make next year the most awesome year ever and everyone will have tons of fun." He looked around the gym. "You need to vote for Robert Pinsent." He held up his hand and flashed a smile. "Go, Bendale!"

It was possibly the best, whitest-toothed Pinsent smile ever.

I could see the kids around me were impressed.

Pinsent had brought his A-game.

Boris needed an A-plus — or my dream of him getting over 20 percent of the votes was dead.

Boris took the mic from the Principal.

Most of the kids started talking.

"Thanks, Robert. First off, I want to wish you the best of luck. I know that no matter who wins, we'll both work hard to make Bendale a better place."

The kids quieted down a little.

"I don't want to tell anyone how to vote. I mean — you should decide that for yourself."

Things quieted still more.

"I only really want to say one thing: vote for the person you think will work hardest for Bendale, the person who can help the most, who can help all the kids in all the grades have a great year. Maybe that means we change a few things, like maybe more intramurals, doing more for the community, like food drives or cleaning the school up or raising money for charity, and maybe setting up more clubs to give kids stuff to do at lunch or after school. You've seen my posters around and maybe checked out my website for my ideas, so I won't repeat them now. I'm serious about it, and I hope we can get them done.

"You'll tell me what you want to do, and I'll try to do it — with the rest of the student council. Next year at Bendale will be my last — and I want to make it the best year for you guys, not for me. So ... it's okay if you vote for Robert. You should vote for the guy that you think will do his best to make things great for everyone.

"The funny thing is, I learned so much running for council president that even if I lose the election I think I won something. I got to know a bunch of people better, like the kids in the play and the Science Fair, and tons of kids in the primary grades. I found out a lot about how many kids go hungry every day and how we can try and help them. I was part of the protest in the Valley and learned that together we can help the environment. I guess what I learned most is there are a lot of great people here and I need to listen to everyone and not try to do things by myself all the time."

Boris took a moment to collect himself.

"So what I really wanted to say was that no matter who wins, I'm going to be here to help the student council any way I can. Thanks. And thanks for listening to me."

I looked around.

It seemed most of the kids had actually listened. A few even clapped, which was a good sign.

I let myself hope that maybe Boris would crack the 25 percent mark.

The Principal had the mic. "Can the first and second graders stand up, and your teachers will lead you —"

Ms. Crimpet came over and whispered something in his ear.

The Principal looked up at the clock on the wall. "I guess," he said to Ms. Crimpet. "We apparently have a couple of minutes for questions," he said to us. "Hold up your hand if you want to ask one of the candidates something and I'll point to you. Then stand up and ask your question." He looked around. "No questions? Okay."

"I have a question," a quivery voice interrupted.

Brandon stood in the middle of the gym. The Principal bent his neck forward and raised his eyebrows. "What's the question?"

"It's for Robert," Brandon said. "Why have you been tweeting and putting on your Facebook page that Boris didn't go to the tree fort in the Valley and stop the developer from cutting the tree down — that he faked it all? There was a television interview from the night before showing him in the tree fort — and he started tweeting about it and posting pictures on Instagram at least twelve hours before your first tweet."

Robert stared at Brandon. "I — the Valley Monster … I … We're gonna crush it next year." He threw a fist in the air.

"As president of the Green Goblins, I officially take back the Organic Golden Hemp Award," Brandon said to Robert. "And the Green Goblins will officially vote for Boris Snodbuckle."

"All eight of you." Michael laughed. "Big deal."

"It's a big deal that Robert lied about the Valley," Brandon said.

His voice wasn't quivering anymore.

"Thanks for that question," the Principal said uneasily. "So can I have the first graders and —"

"I have a question, too."

Frieda was on her feet.

"Did you fake your Science Fair exhibit?" she said.

"Frieda?" Ms. Crimpet said. "That's a serious accusation."

"Did you?" Frieda said, ignoring Ms. Crimpet.

Robert flashed a toothy grin — not his best, however. "You're crazy. No way."

"Then bring your exhibit to school tomorrow and show me how it works," Frieda said.

"I, er, don't have it anymore," Robert said. "I threw it out."

"Then make it again," Frieda said.

"I d-d-don't have ... time," Robert stammered. "And the Science Fair is over and ... We're gonna ... crush it next year?"

"We should crush you with Stevie and Jonah's can crusher," Frieda said. She cast a ferocious glare at Robert. "I find it interesting that in math class yesterday you couldn't explain the Pythagorean theorem. I also find it interesting that you usually copy off people during math tests. Yet you're able to build a solar-powered trash compactor?" She pointed an accusing finger. "Explain how an inverter converts direct current into alternating current."

"I ... didn't use an inverter," Robert mumbled.

Frieda laughed dismissively. "Solar power without inverters? You're a liar, a fake — a science fake."

She sat down.

And to think I ever compared Frieda to April at the Munch Mart. What bravery. What spirit!

Obviously, I wasn't the only one who'd had suspicions about Robert's Super-Duper Mega-Whooper Trash Compactor.

Ms. Crimpet was looking at Robert strangely, her arms crossed tightly. For the first time, I noticed a bit of Frieda in her!

"And I saw you throw the script at Mr. Hurley's chest!" Stevie was on his feet. "I saw it, and so did everyone else."

"And I saw you put Mr. Hurley's red notebook in Boris's backpack," Jonah said.

Lynda charged at Robert and poked him in the arm. "You're the worst puller in the school, you and your puller friends — and you did nothing to stop the Wedgie War. The Skittle votes for Snodbuckle!"

Her declaration set off a wild chant from the primary grades.

"*B-Ster — B-Ster — B-Ster — B-Ster*."

"Valley Monster, cha-cha-cha," chanted Michael, along with Wong, Henson and Daniels.

Their chant was quickly drowned out by a thundering round of "B-Ster."

Boris elbowed me in the side.

"Bulldog — another successful operation?" he said.

"Definitely, Wet Wipes," I said.

I had a feeling Robert Pinsent and his crew had just been cleaned up.

PART VIII

Operation Gym-Jam

CHAPTER THIRTY-THREE

"Class, please tidy your desks and begin to read your books. We have about fifteen minutes before recess," Ms. Crimpet said.

"Is it okay if we move the meeting in the War Room tonight to seven fifteen? I had an idea for the Science Fair next year and I wanted to run some tests," I whispered to Boris.

"No problem," Boris said.

"Will the window be open or should I knock?"

"You can use the front door."

I looked at him in amazement.

"Since Operation Feed the World, my parents have changed their minds about you."

So much had changed since then — since the election! Brandon had convinced his fellow Green Goblins that Boris's bravery at the Valley deserved recognition, and he was duly awarded the Organic Golden Hemp Award in a moving ceremony under the big maple tree. The artsy kids asked Boris to speak to the Principal about giving Ms. Holmes a chance to direct the play next year — and the Principal agreed. Finally, and incredibly, Boris had organized a patrol of seventh and eighth graders to put an end to the Wedgie War. No kid had been pulled in almost four days.

And even more incredible? Bendale had a new student

council president: Boris Snodbuckle. He'd gotten 96 percent of the votes.

But most incredible of all, the Principal hadn't given us a detention in a week.

The P.A. system crackled. "Attention, students!" Mrs. Brundleford's voice rang out. "We will be having an indoor recess today because of the cold and damp weather. Please stay in your classrooms. Thank you."

"It is a bit chilly outside," Ms. Crimpet said. She rolled her eyes.

Boris was on his feet in an instant. "I met with the Principal yesterday about this. We've had three indoor recesses in a row, and the only reason is that teachers don't want to do yard duty."

"I appreciate your opinion, Boris, but it's not my decision," Ms. Crimpet said.

Boris sat. He seemed to be mulling over a decision in his mind. Our eyes met. "Operation Gym-Jam," he said to me.

"I'm on it, Mr. President."

I held my hand up.

"Yes, Adrian?" Ms. Crimpet said.

"May I get a quick drink of water?"

She granted me permission. I dropped my pencil and poked Brandon in the right calf with it. He slipped his phone to me. At the water fountain, I quickly tapped out a text message:

> Green light for Operation Gym-Jam. Hit gym at 10:32.

David Skuy

Boris and I had found one person in each class with a phone, and this allowed us to have a secret communications system without alerting the teachers or the Principal. I returned to my seat. Boris kept his gaze fixed on the clock. At 10:32 he jumped up. "To the gym, classmates," he cried. "We will not accept indoor recess any longer. Outdoor recess is sacred. We stay in the gym until they let us out!"

He thrust his fist in the air.

The kids let out a mighty roar, rose as one and ran to the stairs.

Ms. Crimpet smiled. "Good luck with the protest, Boris. A little fresh air would do wonders for you all."

"Thanks, Ms. Crimpet," Boris said.

We headed to the staircase. Students were pouring out of every classroom and racing to the gym.

"We might be facing some detentions and probably a suspension," Boris said to me.

"Can't be avoided, I'm afraid," I said. "Rule One of the Code: *Don't break school rules, unless there's a really good reason.*"

We clasped arms.

"Are you going to address the student body?" I said.

"I think I need to," Boris said.

"I prepared a speech if you want to look it over," I said, handing him the file.

Boris didn't open it. "No need," he said. "I trust you."

We stopped at the gym door. Most of the students were already inside.

"The school is with you, Mr. President," I said.

It gave me a great deal of pleasure to call him that.

He'd asked me to stick with Boris or the B-Ster, but I was having trouble doing it.

"As long as you're with me, I got no worries," Boris said. He raised one eyebrow and marched into the gym.

The students broke out into a loud cheer, and a chant of "B-Ster — B-Ster" started up, led by the remarkable Lynda Skittle.

I heard someone approaching the door, and I stepped aside.

"Hi, Adrian," Frieda said.

I waited for my heart to start thumping uncontrollably and for my head to begin spinning. I felt remarkably normal, however. Then a most wonderful thing happened. I thought of something to say.

"Hi, Frieda. Good to see you."

"So what's Operation Gym-Jam?" she asked.

"We've been forced to have indoor recess three days in a row. The weather is not that bad. A raincoat, a hat and maybe a pair of thin gloves are more than enough to keep warm. Boris has organized a sit-in. We don't leave until the Principal lets us out."

Frieda screwed up her eyes and looked into the gym. "Snodbuckle's a good president — best we've ever had. You're good friends, right?"

I answered politely. "I'd like to think we are."

"That's nice ... having friends, I mean. I've always wanted ..." She tucked her hair behind her ears. A finger got caught in a knot and she let out a squeak. "I guess you're going to be busy with the sit-in. I shouldn't bother you."

"You're not bothering me. I don't have to do anything

until the band comes to entertain the students."

"I didn't see you at the last Science Club meeting," Frieda said.

In light of recent events, and the discovery of Robert's lies, the Principal had removed our ban from school clubs. Boris did his best to attend, but he was often too busy with student council duties. I had gone to two meetings.

"I felt bad about missing the last one," I said. "Boris and I had to meet the mayor at City Hall to talk about the new trees we're planting by the swings."

"I can understand that," she said. "You're busy with stuff, friends."

Her tone struck a chord with me. She sounded unhappy.

"What did you discuss at Science Club?" I asked.

"It was unproductive. I wanted to talk about NASA's recent satellite pictures. There was an article in *Science* magazine last week. But everyone voted to have a paper-airplane fight instead."

"I found that article very interesting," I said.

"Do you read *Science*?"

"I try to when I can."

"That's good. Yeah ... Well ... Maybe after school, if you're not too busy, which I'm sure you are, so we should probably forget it, but maybe, after school, we could ..." Frieda's voice trailed off.

"We could meet in the library and discuss the article," I said.

Her smile fired my heart.

"I would like that," she said.

"Me too."

Her face was red. If I didn't know better, I'd say she was embarrassed. I couldn't imagine why.

"That's great," she said. "We can talk about science and ... I wanted to hear more about your science exhibit. I've been doing a lot of reading about solar power recently." She tucked her hair behind her ears again. "We don't have to only talk about science. I mean, there's lots going on at school, and, um ... there's a school dance coming up, for example, which might be fun to go to, if I had a friend to go with."

Frieda looked into my eyes and then shifted her gaze to the wall behind me.

Boris had organized a dance to kick off Operation Bendale Students Help the Community. I'd been to several school dances before. I'd never danced at one, though — certainly not with a girl — and most definitely not with Frieda.

The strangest idea occurred to me. For some reason, I also thought I would enjoy going to the dance.

"If you're not going to the dance with someone else, then I'd be happy to go with you," I said.

"Okay," she said quickly.

We laughed — I'm not sure why we both found that funny, but we did.

"I mean, I'm not going with someone else, so I can go with you," she said.

"I would enjoy that."

The conversation suddenly stopped. I searched for something to say, but words eluded me, and it appeared that Frieda was suffering from the same problem.

"I'll go inside now," Frieda said finally. "Speak to you later."

I held the door open and she went in.

The Adrian Nickels who closed the door was not the same Adrian who had climbed into the War Room so many weeks before to launch Operation S.O.S. This election had taught me a few things.

Don't give up, believe in yourself, be brave and sometimes — sometimes — good things happen. And if you want to ask a girl to a dance, then you should.

I went into the gym. Boris had taken the stage. He held a microphone.

"Students of Bendale," he said. "The Principal thinks he can lock us up all day in this school and never let us out because there's a chill in the air. He thinks he can cancel outdoor recess anytime he wants. Well, he's wrong. I asked him yesterday to let us out, rain or shine. He obviously won't listen. We have to make him listen. I say we don't leave this gym until he lets us have our recess. Are you with me, Bendale?"

The students let out a cheer.

"In five minutes a band is coming to play for us," Boris said. "If the Principal won't let us have fun at recess, we'll make our own fun."

The cheer was twice as loud this time.